ASCENSION

BOOK ONE OF THE ASCENSION SERIES

LAURA HALL

COPYRIGHT

Editing by *Lawrence Editing*

AS · CEN · SION

| əˈsenSHən | noun [in sing.]

: the act of rising or ascending;
: the act of moving to a higher or more powerful
position.

PROLOGUE

THE APOCALYPSE DIDN'T GO AS EXPECTED. No volcanic eruptions or tidal waves. No asteroid, aliens, or celestial horsemen.

That's not to say it wasn't bad.

It was devastating.

Two years after the fateful day that changed the world, the remaining powers-that-be named the event Ascension. The intent was for a literal interpretation, but someone didn't do their research.

For those who'd been struggling with the spiritual implications of the event, it cemented the belief they'd been left behind. In the following months, mass suicides happened on the regular. By the time discussions began to find a new moniker, it was too late. Ascension had stuck.

As far as I knew, no one actually went anywhere

in an esoteric sense. Not unless those who died—horribly and painfully—caught piggyback rides on angels' wings when no one was watching. Granted, we were all a little distracted.

There were riots, fires, and food and water shortages lasting months. It took more than five years for the wildly swinging pendulum of normalcy to find balance on its newly fashioned scale. Now, fourteen years after Ascension, we're finally—mostly—there.

The New Normal.

Funny how the passage of years will shift perspective and how adaptable the human species is when faced with reality-bending circumstance. What once seemed so catastrophic is now a worldwide holiday, celebrated with festivals, retail markdowns, and used car tent sales.

July 28. Ascension Day.

Or, in more personal terms: The Day Fifty Million People Died.

Scientists have spent the last decade-plus trying to figure out why, out of the blue, all human brains on the planet decided to change over the course of a day. And why did the sudden activity in formerly quiescent gray matter kill so many? For that matter, why did our brains alter our bodies' abilities to procreate and age, and for a good many, radically alter DNA?

Numerous theories have arisen over the years, but no definitive answers. None that satisfy the scientists among us, anyway. The truth is, no one knows what happened, or in what order. It's a Chicken and Egg quandary.

Was it an environmental factor, or more plausibly, multiple factors, that spontaneously altered our DNA, which in turn woke up portions of our sleeping minds?

Or did some evolutionary trigger in our brains depress, which then prompted cellular mutations?

Was it environmental, biological, or circumstantial? Was it biowarfare gone wrong? (Denials all around on that one).

And why the hell did it happen exclusively on July 28?

Before Ascension, I was a Statistician. My master's thesis had to do with predicting ovarian cancer survival rates, which landed me a dream job out of college at Cedars-Sinai in Los Angeles.

Fortunately for humanity, cancer is no longer a global health issue. Ascension took care of it and, consequently, my job.

Like millions of others, I lost my way post-Ascension. Part of the problem was the interminable future stretching before me. Fourteen years after the fact, I still see the same twenty-eight-year-old face and body in my mirror.

If I avoid a lethal accident, there's no telling how long it will take me to grow old. Me and everyone else. Well, everyone except the elderly. They were stuck with the short end of the everlasting-life stick; although we were all revitalized internally, external appearances have remained the same. Science now tells us that we're still aging. We'll still die. Just not for a long, long time.

We've all had adjusting to do.

Only children have continued aging at normal rates, though it's been shown that their growth plateaus around the quarter-century mark. The only infants born since Ascension were those already conceived, and no new pregnancies have been documented. Zero human births, whereas animals are procreating just fine.

Scientists are working on that mystery, too.

My current avenue of life, according to my dad, is more like an alleyway to nowhere. I work part-time in my uncle Mal's pub in Los Angeles and do taxes on the side.

Yes, we still have taxes. Democrats and Republicans. The House, Senate, and Supreme Court. Minimum wage and welfare. Healthcare took a big hit, as the need for it radically declined post-Ascension. Cedars-Sinai is still open, but UCLA Medical Center is now UCLA Learning Center for Magic Users.

Despite the chaos that followed Ascension, not much has changed in terms of societal structure. People are still assholes. Capitalism is alive and well. And yet, everything is different.

For starters, the President of the United States is a werewolf.

1

IT WAS a typical Friday night at Sullivan's Pub in Silver Lake. The atmosphere was purposefully dim, with rock music providing a frenetic backdrop to an old, familiar story: a bar full of women and the men trying to go home with them.

I'd like to say that when the rest of our brains came online, emotional IQs increased exponentially, leading us to seek more meaningful, lasting relationships. Not so much. If anything, the lack of STDs and accidental pregnancies have made casual sex disturbingly conventional.

Founded by my uncle Mal over thirty years ago, Sullivan's was a neighborhood fixture long before Silver Lake turned trendy. Over the years, the crowd has evolved from blue collar workers and biker outlaws to trendsetters, artists, and the young entrepreneurial crowd.

"A Manhattan, please."

I nodded at my customer and poured the drink, then carefully traded booze for cash across the counter. "Change?" I asked, glancing up from the bill in my fingers.

He shook his head, sending shaggy blond hair flying. Even without the dog-like wiggle and yellowish tinge in his otherwise brown eyes, I knew he was a shifter. Given the area, most likely coyote. His aura was a weak pulse—definitely low on the alpha scale.

"What's with the white streak in your hair?" he asked.

I closed the cash drawer, keeping my fingers away from the metal sides. "Stuck my finger in a light socket."

The shifter smiled, displaying slightly elongated teeth, an indication of too much time spent in his other body. If he stayed in human form, the effect would fade in a few days. I had a feeling that wouldn't be the case with this guy.

Undeterred by my dismissive vibe, he continued, "What's your name?"

I swallowed a sigh and glanced down the length of the bar, sizing up drinks and customers. Katrina, my usual scapegoat, was at the other end dealing with a couple of vampires pissed that we were out of O-Neg. To my chagrin, no one needed my immediate attention.

I answered shortly, "Fiona."

"Hi, Fiona, I'm Eddie."

He stuck out his hand for me to shake. I ignored it. Maybe he meant well, but I was just jaded enough to suspect he didn't. This wasn't my first rodeo.

"Nice to meet you, Eddie. Enjoy your drink." Hoping he took the hint, I turned my back to the counter and began restocking pint glasses.

"Told you she'd burn you, dude," slurred a voice behind me. "You owe me twenty bucks."

"Shit," groaned Eddie.

I glanced aside to find Katrina watching me. She rolled her eyes and mouthed, "Assholes." I nodded and went back to work, well aware of my reputation as a prude and completely fine with it.

Twenty minutes later there was another contender, this time an Amber mage whose power was a dim orange flare around his shoulders. He didn't bother with flattery, going straight for the money-shot.

"So, what are you? Cipher or null?"

It was the million-dollar question. They were the

only two options for me, seeing as I didn't turn furry, drink blood, or cast spells.

Ciphers, accounting for 18.3 percent of the population, were humans who had come through Ascension more or less unchanged, save an imbedded defense system toward supernaturals. Vampires couldn't work mind control over them. Shifters couldn't infect them with a bite. No matter what a mage threw at a cipher, they remained untouched.

Nulls, on the other hand, were humans for whom Ascension was a passing, uneventful storm. No changes. No powers. Just a headache that lasted most of the day. They comprised only 8.5 percent of the population worldwide and even less, 4 percent, in the United States. Most nulls stayed away from the heavily supernatural city centers, preferring communal living in rural areas. I didn't blame them. Those who stayed, less than 1 percent, invariably hired mages to work protection spells over them, giving them almost the same level of immunity as ciphers.

But I wasn't a cipher or a null.

Lucky for me, my uncle Mal was kind of a badass, a mage whose power was a vibrant blue nimbus. Long ago, he'd embedded spells in the skin of my arms. They weren't inherently defensive, as we'd discovered I was mostly immune to mind control, but served another, dual purpose. The snaking vines of text obscured the narrow ribbons of white scarring on my arms, bolstering my self-control while simultaneously projecting a subliminal warning to those around me.

Off-Limits. Do Not Touch.

Most of the time, the spells worked. But humans, Ascended or not, were stubborn and arrogant. They didn't like mysteries. Didn't like *other*. When, two years ago, a troll had crawled out from under the Brooklyn Bridge, the poor guy had been shot at, hit with cars, and set on fire. It had taken a hundred police, acting on orders from the president, to isolate and thereby protect the ancient, albeit naïve beastie.

Unsurprisingly, no other fairytale creatures have come out of the woodwork since.

"So?" pressed the mage. "Cipher or null?"

From behind me, Katrina snarled, "That's none of your business."

The mage scowled. "No need to bite my head off, kitten."

The moniker was a mistake. With one long-legged stride, Katrina was halfway across the counter and had the mage's collar in her hands—her abruptly claw-tipped hands. With a notable growl in her tone, she said, "Call me kitten again."

The customers to either side began edging away, which was smart of them. I wondered where Mal was. If he was watching.

"I-I meant no offense," gasped the mage. For a few moments, he struggled futilely against her hold. Then he tried another angle, turning wide eyes to me. "I'm sorry. Really. My bad."

The warm, familiar weight of a large hand settled on my shoulder. As it belonged to the man who'd set the spells on me, he was unaffected by the resulting electrical surge. The deep blue radiance of his aura filled my peripheral vision, undetectable to all but me.

Uncle Mal said calmly, "Let him go, Katrina." She did, tossing blond hair over her shoulder as she sauntered to the other end of the bar. The accosted mage blinked at Mal, clearly uncertain as to whether he should offer thanks or apology. I could have told him which, but kept my mouth shut.

"How much?" asked Mal.

Another owl-like blink from the mage. "What?"

The jewel-toned light grew more pronounced, now visible to anyone looking our way. Mal didn't often show his true colors, but when he did, people noticed.

A sapphire aura signified a high ranking mage, one who didn't need preparation or tools to enact spells, just words and gestures. The only level of mastery above Sapphire was Opal, denoting a mage who could trigger a spell with a thought. There were only five Opal Mages in the U.S., and four of them were government employees.

Sapphire Mages weren't as rare as Opals, but they were rare enough. Since undergoing his mandatory training ten years ago, Mal had been approached no less than twenty times by various government agencies. He always turned them down.

In a low, dangerous tone, he asked, "How big is the betting pool on whether Fiona is a cipher or a null?"

The lesser mage blanched, stumbled off his stool, and disappeared into the crowd.

"It's okay, Mal," I said softly.

He grunted at my lie. It wasn't okay and we both knew it. Exposure as something other than the acceptable classes was a fear I carried every day. It was so much a part of me that it was a dull ache, like the back pain I'd had pre-Ascension.

When the first mandatory Census happened two years post-Ascension, I'd managed to pass as a cipher with Mal's help. The tests were much more rigorous these days. Past-due notices to renew my registration were piling up in a junk drawer at home.

Eventually, someone would come looking for me.

When they found me, I had no doubt the rest of my life would be spent in an underground testing facility somewhere. Probably with the Brooklyn troll for a cellmate. The media line was that he'd vanished without a trace from FBI headquarters in New York.

Riiight.

"What are we going to do?" I murmured, turning to look up at my uncle. He was stuck in his early sixties, with one of those faces that reached peak attractiveness in middle age. Coupled with a full head of chestnut hair and sparkling hazel eyes, my uncle had no problems with the ladies.

Right now, his eyes were worried. More worried than I'd seen them since the early years, when he and my father had resorted to keeping me in a basement until I could manage my ability. For my own safety and theirs.

Except for my brief, stress-ridden foray to the local Census Department, I'd spent the majority of six years underground, a veritable live wire with perpetually singed-off hair, until both my hard won control and Mal's spellwork had earned me reintroduction to the world.

I was struggling with control right now, which probably accounted for the concerned frown on Mal's face. It'd been a long day and I hadn't slept well last night, two key ingredients in my personal recipe for disaster.

Tiny, electrical pulses traveled the scars on my arms, triggering a powerful itching in my palms. My long-sleeved shirt began to heat, chafing my sensitive skin. I sucked air through my teeth and closed my eyes. *Relax. Relax.*

Mal squeezed my shoulder. "Take a break," he ground out.

No need to tell me twice. Ducking past him, I made a beeline for freedom, sidling past customers and down a short hallway to the back door. The metal bar depressed at my touch, throwing a thick spark that was thankfully blocked by my body.

I stepped into the mild September evening, letting the door slam closed. The alleyway was blessedly empty of humanity. Just me, two ripe dumpsters, and scurrying rats.

Crouching, I slammed my palms into the asphalt and released the charge in my body. The current happily complied, pulsing outward in ever weakening cycles, until, finally, I was back to normal.

Whatever normal was.

2

THE DREAM WAS ALWAYS the same. It began with the smell of campfire smoke and s'mores, and dry California air flavored with pine resin. Then followed sensation. A whisper of breeze across my bare arms. Michael's warm fingers tracing patterns on the back of my neck. Warmth in my chest that reflected the moment.

Happiness. Belonging.

It was July 27. We were camping in the Angeles National forest, my fiancé and I, along with our good friends Sally and Mason Montgomery. It was nearing midnight, and we'd settled in chairs around the crackling fire with plastic cups of wine.

We were laughing at something Mason said when midnight struck.

Light. Heat. Concussion.

Darkness.

I woke up in the woods, covered in dirt and vomit. My arms were scorched from shoulders to the tips of my fingers, the skin peeling off in blackened strips. The pain was a distant feeling, insulated by a strange humming in my bones.

I screamed for Michael until I grew hoarse, until feeling returned to my legs. The night was moonless, the forest unnaturally silent, but like a compass needle drawn to magnetic north, I stumbled straight back to camp.

All that remained of our site was a huge, steaming crater, the epicenter of which was my melted camping chair. Strewn around the hole were body parts. Bits and pieces, strangely bloodless. Sally's head. Mason's arms and legs. Michael's glasses, the surfaces cracked, obscuring his dead eyes.

The humming noise increased to a ring.

A shrill, incessant ring...

The dream shattered as I opened my eyes, blinking into the morning light. On my nightstand, my cell phone continued trilling. I wiped the wetness from my face, hissing as sparks flew between my fingertips and my tears. Neither could hurt me, but both were damned annoying.

Rolling into a sitting position, I dropped my feet

to the floor to ground my charge, then reached for the phone. It took a few seconds of staring blankly at the screen, but eventually the wavering letters of a name took shape.

"Uncle Mal?" I croaked.

His gravelly voice boomed out, "When was the last time you heard from your father?"

I shook my head the rest of the way into wakefulness. "Um… a couple of days ago. He said he was going out of town on a case."

"What case?"

I blinked in surprise. As a rule, Mal and my father, Frank, showed zero interest in each other's businesses. Mal thought my father was a fool for leaving the LAPD seven years ago to start a private investigations firm. My father thought Mal was wasting his talents running a bar when he could be *making a difference.*

When the men were in the same room together, I was never more grateful for being an only child.

"I don't know," I told him. "When we had lunch last week he was tight-lipped about it. What's going on?"

His silence lasted a beat too long, like he was debating how much to tell me. A queer, sinking feeling seized my stomach.

Finally, he said, "I got a call from the security

company that patrols his office building. I'm here now. It looks like Bigfoot went on a rampage."

I shot to my feet in alarm. "What? Why did the security company call you?"

"Frank put me down as the secondary contact. Probably meant it as a joke." He paused for a slow breath. "I think you should come down here, kiddo."

Balancing the phone between my shoulder and ear, I yanked on last night's jeans. "Where's Rosie? Is she there?"

"Rosie? Oh, right, the secretary he can't afford. Nope."

I yanked off my camisole and lunged for the bra hanging from my bedpost. "Okay, I'll call her on my way over. When was the last time you tried Dad?"

"Right before I called you. Straight to voicemail."

Those three words ramped me from worried to freaked-the-hell-out. My father's cell phone stayed within two feet of him at all times, a habit from his days as a detective. He had backup batteries and a phone charger in every corner of his house and office. There was no way he'd left town without provisioning accordingly.

The phone began heating against my ear. I quickly grounded my charge as Mal said gruffly, "Just get over here."

"Ten minutes," I said and hung up.

SULLIVAN INVESTIGATIONS WAS IN BURBANK, in a dumpy stucco building with peeling terra-cotta paint and sagging wood trim. My father's lack of success as a P.I. wasn't because Los Angeles didn't have a need for skilled investigators, or that crime had miraculously diminished post-Ascension.

The reality was that my father, bleeding heart werebear that he was, had a hard time taking money from his clients. There were occasions—like today— that I agreed with Mal's assessment of his career choice. Being an LAPD detective wasn't the safest work, but at least it came with a paycheck and lots of backup when shit hit the fan.

I parked in the small lot between Mal's truck and Rosie's beat-up Civic, then jogged up cement stairs to the second floor. My dad's office was the corner unit by the street, boasting a charming view of traffic and one tired palm tree.

Mal stood outside the door, which, as I drew closer, appeared to be a twisted hunk of metal and broken glass.

"Holy shit."

He nodded perfunctorily and growled, "Mind the glass," before disappearing inside.

I stepped carefully—flip-flops had clearly been

a mistake—and walked into what looked like a bombed out building in a war zone. Beside the untouched window with its aforementioned view, there was a jagged hole in the wall roughly the size of a basketball. Weak sunlight filtered through the breach and plaster dust hung in the air like a haze. I looked around, my mind skipping details in order to take in the bigger picture.

Destruction.

"Where are the cops?" I asked, my voice small.

"I wanted to look around before I called them."

I shook my head helplessly. "Why? Where's Rosie?"

A dark eyebrow rose. "Didn't you call her?"

My stomach clenched. "She didn't answer. Her car's outside, though. Oh, God. What if she was here? What if something's happened to her?"

Mal was across the room in seconds, his hands slamming onto my shoulders. Electricity bottomed out through my feet with an audible *snap*.

"Sorry," I whispered.

He released me to rub his palms over his face. "No, I'm sorry." He dropped his hands to stare at me. "Your power is outgrowing my spells again."

For some inexplicable reason, in the last year my voltage had been increasing. The growth spurts were random, undetectable until something set me off, and always scary.

We didn't talk about it, but both Mal and I knew there would come a time when even his skills would fail to protect me. Or, more importantly, someone else.

"Can you redo them? Even stronger?"

He grimaced. "I have and did. Last night, and again just now. You're neutralizing them faster than I can rebuild."

I blinked dry eyes and refocused on the warped metal blob that had been my father's desk. My lightning-rod issues would have to wait in line.

Clearing my throat, I told him, "I called dad and left a message. Maybe he got sidetracked somewhere without service." I didn't believe it, but it was all I could come up with.

Mal's gaze was heavy on my face, but he finally cosigned my redirection. "Maybe."

He walked across the debris-strewn floor to the only untouched fixture in the room: a stacked filing cabinet. With a pass of his broad hand over the top, runes began glowing on the dull gray surface.

"Open."

Click.

He pulled out the top drawer and began rummaging through files, muttering about what a disorganized ass his brother was. I spent the time taking a longer look around, with no idea what I was looking for. There didn't seem to be any rhyme or reason to the ruin.

"It looks like a mage threw a hissy fit," I said.

Mal grunted. "Do you sense anything?"

As a part of my personal Ascension goody bag, I could sense and sometimes see the auras of supernaturals. Vamp auras felt like cool, tickling wind, shifters like a pulse. Only the auras of mages were visible and colorful, reflecting their level of power.

Occasionally, too, I could pick up on residual energies in a space once the owner was gone. Resonance, Mal called it. But only if the subject was powerful. An old vamp, an alpha shifter, or a mage ranked Emerald or higher.

I let my eyes unfocus a bit and scanned the room, then shook my head. Just Mal's aura and dust motes.

"No, I don't." I glanced at the warped desk. "You think it was a shifter?"

"Nope."

My palms tingled and I curled my fingers into fists. "What, then?"

The file drawer slammed closed. Mal glanced up from the thick folder in his hands, wearing an expression I'd never seen before. It made my blood run cold. His gaze swept the office.

"We have to get out of here. Now."

"Wha—wait!"

Ignoring my protest, he dragged me by the arm toward the door. We were two steps away when a *boom* rocked the space. I was ripped away from him, my body forced backward until my spine slammed against the opposite wall. My head hit last, hard enough for stars to dance in my vision.

I tried to reach up, to cradle my throbbing skull, but my fingers barely twitched. I was glued to the wall like an insect to flypaper.

Mal was faring slightly better. He battled an invisible foe in the center of the room, a sapphire glow around him. His arms were outstretched toward the empty doorway, his lips moving though I couldn't hear words. Magic saturated the air, suffocating in its density.

The folder from the filing cabinet had fallen, papers and photographs scattering across the floor. I watched one photo flutter and finally come to rest, face-up, near my bare feet.

At first glance the image appeared abstract, predominantly red and white. But upon closer examination, I was forced to concede that my mind had been protecting me. It was a body. A mutilated, half-furry body strapped to… *Was that an electric chair?*

"Cease!" cried a deep, stern voice.

Not Mal's.

I watched helplessly as my uncle's arms fell to his sides. He was breathing heavily, sweat soaking through his gray T-shirt. The shock was wearing off, and my lungs began heaving with panic. I struggled against my invisible bonds.

"Calm down, Fiona," murmured Mal, just as a shadow moved into the doorway. A man, average in height and slender, with short blond hair, stepped into the office. Even before I saw his milky eyes, I saw the white robes, and knew.

Opal Mage.

Which meant…

Another figure appeared, striding gracefully around his partner. Dressed in a fine Italian suit, which fit his tall, leanly muscled form to perfection, the Prime of the Western United States fixed bright green eyes on Mal.

"It's been a long time, Malcolm."

Oh, fuck.

3

THERE WERE FOUR PRIMES, three men and a woman, all vampires. Old vamps, the kind who'd been sucking blood for centuries. When Ascension hit, approximately one third of the Ancients died, while the rest awoke with the greatest gift a vampire could receive: immunity to sunlight. No such luck for the humans turned into vampires by the DNA scramble of Ascension. They were still stuck in the dark.

In the early years, I'd been too busy grieving and throwing sparks to monitor the Primes' rise to the political stage. Apparently, they'd been of invaluable service to the White House in the turmoil following Ascension. I dimly remember hearing about them quelling riots and halting assassination attempts, and later spearheading the Census. There was also the matter of national security. Put simply, they secured it.

Each of the Primes oversaw a multi-state region. West, Midwest, South, and Northeast. To satisfy would-be antagonists, they worked in a democratic triumvirate with an Alpha and Omega. The Alpha, no surprise, was an alpha shifter. And the Omega was an Opal Mage.

The triumvirates were responsible for registering and monitoring all supernaturals in their zones. They settled territory disputes between rival shifter packs, monitored vampire nests and the masters who ran them, and enforced strict ethical regulations on magic users.

If local police couldn't handle a rogue shifter, or a rampaging mage, they called their Prime's office. And when it came to punishment, the Primes had carte blanche from the president to imprison or execute as they saw fit. Medieval. But effective.

Because of the Primes, the United States quickly regained its superpower status post-Ascension. Not so for many other countries, where supernatural factions continued to wage bloody battles for supremacy.

The Western Prime was the oldest of the four, and there was speculation he was the most powerful vamp in the world. Rumor also had it he was a longtime friend of the president, Randolph Brant, now in his second term.

The Prime's advocates wanted him to run for the Oval Office in two years. His most outspoken critics called him a manipulative mastermind and accused the president of being in his pocket.

Politics aside, I was well and truly screwed.

"Prime Thorne," said Mal in an mild tone. "Sorry about the misunderstanding. Thought you were someone else."

"Really, Malcolm, call me Connor. We've known each other long enough." Keenly intelligent green eyes, the color of spring grass, surveyed the ruined office. When they passed over me, I flinched and looked down. "Where's Frank?"

"Out of town."

A shifting of robes had me glancing up to see the Omega stepping to the Prime's side. The mage's eyes were no longer white but a rich, limpid brown. Without the freaky orbs, he looked young and approachable, like a fresh-faced college student. Except for the robes, which were just weird.

"No magic besides Malcolm's," murmured the mage, "but something doesn't feel right."

"Alchemy," said Mal.

The Omega stiffened, worry aging his face ten

years. "Of course. Thank you. I failed to recognize it."

I had no idea what alchemy was, but the easy way the Omega admitted ignorance had me warming toward him. Maybe someday I'd forgive him for slamming me into a wall. If he ever unsealed me from it.

The Prime focused on my uncle, a frown pinching the skin between dark brows. "Frank Sullivan was due in Seattle two days ago. He never arrived."

I tried putting two and two together but kept coming up with five. *No way*. There was no way my dad had been flying to Seattle to meet with the Western Prime. Not without telling me.

My gaze jerked to Mal. He looked similarly shocked, his mouth hanging open.

With all the incredulity I felt, he barked, "He was meeting *you?*"

The Prime nodded distractedly as he once more gazed around the room. I had my first full look at his face without the filter of a magazine page or television screen. My thoughts scattered, my heart pumping a little faster.

Classic features à la ancient battlefields, midnight rituals, and dark, lush forests. Pale skin with an undertone of gold, dark hair with a hint of curl. A tapering jaw, chiseled cheekbones, wide eyes, and a smooth brow.

As if that wasn't enough, as a vampire he had that extra *something* that elevated him from handsome to beautiful. Something that made you look twice, then keep staring until he either passed out of sight or you drooled all over your shoes.

"This is Frank's daughter, I presume?"

The voice shocked me out of a daydream starring the Prime, a gladiator costume, and rivulets of sweat. My heart slammed against my ribs and I looked at Mal, who was glaring at me. I glared back. It wasn't my fault the Prime's glamour had bulldozed my natural defenses. He was freaking *ancient*.

"She's bleeding, Connor," said the Omega.

It sounded like a warning, though the Prime didn't heed it. He picked his way through the rubble until he stood before me. My eyes instinctively found his. At the contact, his power unfurled, dark and drugging, pulling air from my lungs in a gasp.

"Let her go, Adam."

"Connor—"

"Do it."

The invisible bindings dissolved, dropping my full weight onto the glass beneath my feet. I hissed in pain, the Prime recoiled, and Mal grabbed my arm as electricity surged. Apparently, the Omega's spell had been keeping my power at bay.

My uncle groaned as he took the first heavy pulse of energy.

"What—" began the Omega. "Connor, no!"

Cool fingers seized my other hand and my vision went dark.

AWARENESS RETURNED SLOWLY. I had to work for it, trudging up a subconscious stairwell with leaden limbs. My eyelids opened with effort, parting sticky eyelashes to present me with a coffered ceiling of pale taupe.

Directly above the bed in which I lay hung a tiered chandelier, its many bulbs radiating soft light through an ornate hotel bedroom. Heavy curtains blocked windows opposite the bed, but I had an indefinable sense that I was high up, closer than usual to the clouds.

My skin was itchy, uncomfortable. My arms felt numb. I clenched my fingers, which felt like limp noodles.

Something was seriously wrong. With the level of anxiety and gut-liquefying fear I felt, I should be throwing sparks like a firecracker.

"You're awake."

I jerked, whipping my head around on the pillow to see the Omega seated in a chair beside the bed. He watched me with narrowed eyes. They were currently brown, though the sight didn't comfort. Not when, like all Opals, he could kill with a thought.

Luckily for everyone on the planet, when it came to Opals, Nature made an effort to balance the scales. There were so few of them because they tended to kill themselves within a year of transition, sometimes taking small populations with them.

Another lesson hammered home by Ascension: too much power made people crazy. Especially power over life and death.

I ran a thick tongue along the back of my teeth. My mouth tasted like firewood. "Where am I?" I asked hoarsely. "Where's Mal?"

"He's with the Prime. I'm Adam Gibbs, by the way."

God, he looked young. Early twenties, maybe, at Ascension. Despite intellectually knowing he was pushing toward his forties, the baby face was throwing me for a loop.

"Don't hurt him," I said. "I'll do whatever you want."

The Omega blinked, lips pinching. "Why would we hurt Malcolm?"

I frowned, nonplussed, and finally shook my head. "Can I see my uncle? I won't do anything, I swear."

A small, tired smile lifted his mouth. "You've already done plenty." I tried to sit up, but found myself unable to move. Again. "Don't struggle. It will only agitate you."

I dropped my head back to the pillow. Squeezing my eyes shut, I asked, "What did I do? Did I hurt Mal?" Then I remembered who else had touched me mid-surge. "Oh God, is Prime Thorne okay?"

"He's fine," said a new voice, low and lightly ironic.

I opened my eyes to see the man himself standing behind Adam's chair and looking completely at ease, even humored. His eyes met mine and I glanced away before I could be sucked back into them.

Maybe, if I asked nicely, they'd let me see my dad and uncle a final time.

"You're not going to die," said the Prime, still in that vaguely amused tone. "Not by my hand, at least. And you certainly aren't going to be shipped off to a prison cell." He paused. "Really, Adam, we need to do something about those rumors. It was only the one facility years ago, and we shut it down."

Adam sighed, robes rustling as he stood. "We can't blame her for being afraid. Our nation doesn't have the strongest track record of tolerance."

The Prime made a noncommittal noise.

I tried to think of nothing, which only opened the door for a confusing jumble of images. Witches burning at the stake. Lab rats and the furry, mutilated body in that photograph.

The fact that the Prime had access to my every thought made me twitch with discomfort. Especially when the damned image of him in gladiator finery popped up. My mortification was complete when I heard his low chuckle.

Steeling myself, I dragged my gaze back to him. He'd taken the Omega's seat. The mage now paced near the bedroom doorway, fingers tapping on his cell phone.

"Hello, Fiona. I'm Connor."

My name in his mouth was unsettlingly intimate. Ignoring the reactionary heat in my face, I stared at his nose, which looked like it had been broken once or twice in his human years.

"Nice to meet you, Prime Thorne. How long are you going to keep me like this?"

He ignored my question, instead leaning forward to brace elbows on his knees. His gaze trailed down my arms, exposed without the light jacket I'd been wearing earlier.

"Fascinating," he murmured, a banked glow flashing in his eyes. He glanced up, focusing on the white streak in my otherwise dark hair. "Tell me of your Ascension."

There was no point in lying.

"I was struck by lightning."

He sat back, sending a quick glance across the room. Adam looked up from his phone and said, "There were several hundred reported cases of lightning striking people at midnight. None in which the affected survived, though."

The thought of Michael was instinctive. I couldn't stop it any more than I could will myself to stop breathing. I closed my eyes, not wanting to see the Prime's expression as I thought of my dead fiancé.

There was a heavy moment of silence, then cool fingertips grazed my forehead.

"Sleep," said the Prime.

I did.

4

THE SUN BLAZED MERRILY in an azure sky, showering the world with heat and light and refracting off the pale sand beneath my feet. Shading my face with a hand, I gazed through watering eyes at my dreamworld.

It was the Roman Colosseum. Not as it was today, an impressive shadow of former greatness, but whole. The hundreds of elegant travertine arches, richly engraved columns, and rows upon rows of tiered seating were a feast of geometric beauty.

"Lovely, isn't it?" asked a low voice.

As I turned, clouds moved over the sun and dappled shadows raced across the sand. I regarded the Western Prime, standing some ten feet away, and realized two things. One, if this were my dream, he'd be wearing a loincloth instead of his fancy suit. And two, the detail around me was much too involved for my imagination to have conjured.

"What is this place?" I asked and immediately wanted to slap myself.

"The Colosseum," he said with a twitch of lips. I flushed, dropping my gaze to his feet. "If you're wondering whether you're dreaming, the answer is no. But you are unconscious. Do you see the haze in your peripheral vision?"

Only when he mentioned it did I see it—a white radiance, dense and sparkling.

Magic.

I swallowed thickly. "The Omega is doing this?"

"Not exactly." Prime Thorne shrugged out of his suit jacket and tossed it to the sand, then began working to loosen his tie. "You're in my mind. But Adam is near, as is your uncle. They will prevent any spillover that might occur as I test you."

"What do you mean, test me?"

Fingers paused on the button at his neck. His head came up, revealing an expression I associated with teachers the world over: long-suffering patience.

"Don't be afraid. This is a simple exercise to test the scope of your ability. Your uncle underwent a similar trial during his training."

Don't be afraid.

Strangely, I wasn't afraid. Or not so strangely, given that the king of mind-fucking was standing ten feet away. He stopped after two shirt buttons, which I found disappointing, and subsequently unnerving. Hell-bent on ignoring the swath of golden, toned skin from his throat to chest, I stared avidly at his bare feet.

Bouncing lightly, he gave me a come-hither gesture. "I'm ready, Fiona."

I shifted my weight, wondering what I was supposed to do. Did he seriously want me to zap him? I wasn't sure I could. For the first time in recent memory, I didn't feel a charge trying to escape my skin. Maybe it was because I wasn't physically here.

"Stop dallying."

His voice came from behind me. *Right* behind me. I yelped and spun, backpedaling away from him. My heart pounded in my chest, sending furious *Flight! Flight!* messages to my legs. My muscles bunched.

"Do. Not. Run."

The words froze me where I stood, my body poised on the brink of launching into a sprint. It wasn't the authority in his voice that got me—it was the hunger.

The sun rained down its sweltering heat. Sweat beaded on my face and chest. Fear prickled across my scalp as I realized that, pseudo-dream-state or not, I was alone with a predator.

The predator.

Top of the fucking food chain.

"Shit," I whispered, turning slowly to face him.

Pearly fangs glinted as he smiled slightly. "Good girl," he murmured.

Then, like the prey I was, I made the mistake of looking into his eyes. They weren't beautiful anymore, the irises no longer green but glistening obsidian. The sight was too much. Talons of fear pierced my brain. Adrenaline surged in my limbs.

I ran.

I made it maybe five feet before fingers seized my shoulders. My back slammed against a hard chest and my head was wrenched to the side. I screamed and thrashed and swung my legs, none of which did anything except invite a thickly muscled arm around me, trapping my arms to my waist. I was lifted from the ground, all five-foot-seven inches of me. Like I was a doll. Or dinner.

Cool lips traced my jugular, unfazed by the storm of tiny electrical currents erupting from my skin. His strength was inviolable. Barring a miracle, I was going to be bitten by a vampire.

I stilled, quivering, and cursed Fate, the bitch who'd decided that the first lips to touch me in fourteen years would belong to a bloodsucking fiend.

The sudden absence of his grip had me falling forward. My knees slammed into dense sand. Momentum carried me onto my hands, where I stayed, heaving, until the urge to vomit passed.

"Please accept my apologies, Ms. Sullivan."

I almost didn't hear him over the rush of blood in my ears. When the words registered, and I understood that he had been privy to my thought— and released me like a leper because of it—a rush of shame overtook me.

"Screw you," I said and shoved to my feet.

Dark brows rose in surprise over eyes that were green again, though darker than their usual shade. "Excuse me?"

"You heard me."

Anger was accomplishing what fear had failed to. My arms pulsed with heat, the snaking ribbons of scar tissue writhing with silver luminosity. For once, I didn't try to dampen the rise of power. There was no need to ground the charge, only direct it.

At him.

"Do it," he said.

"With pleasure."

I lifted my hands and lightning erupted, arching

brilliant white across the sand and striking the Western Prime in the center of his chest.

Heat.

Light.

Darkness.

And in the darkness, low voices murmured.

"...never seen anything quite like it."

"That was supremely foolish, Connor. What if it had happened in truth?"

A low chuckle, full of genuine mirth. "I might risk it. Such an extraordinary feeling..." The sound of footsteps moving away, then, "And the spell we talked about?"

"Almost done."

When I next opened my eyes, I was in my own bed. I sat up fast, then flopped back down as nausea gripped me. A strange pulse of heat in my body was followed by a wave of cold that made my teeth chatter. Groaning, I lifted a hand to my face, which was flushed and damp with sweat.

"Hey, kiddo."

"Mal," I whispered. The bed depressed by my hip and something cool and wet covered my forehead. It was such a relief that tears stung my eyes. "What's happening to me?"

"You have a fever, but it's passing. You did well.

You held your own against two of the scariest fuckers out there. Proud of you."

My chest squeezed with mingled pride and humiliation. "Couldn't stop him."

"Honey, there's a good reason why you've been kept unconscious all day. Now, I need you to listen carefully. I'm going to find your father, but in order to do that, I need to know you'll be safe. I made a deal with the Prime. My help for your safety."

"No," I breathed out. "Staying with you."

Mal lifted the washcloth and gently wiped my face. "I'd never forgive myself if something happened to you, Fiona. This isn't a negotiation. You're leaving for Seattle with the Prime."

My skin prickled all over. Fever or fear, it was hard to tell. "Not going."

"I'm sorry," whispered Mal, and then more loudly, "Go ahead, Adam." I jerked, but Mal's hand pressed against my chest, holding me down. "It's for the flight, kiddo. Just relax."

"Wha—"

Something sharp pierced my arm.

Darkness.

5

CROSSING the bridge from sleep to waking, I first noticed the scent of flowers. Gardenia, if I wasn't mistaken. Another minute and my heavy eyelids parted on a new ceiling, this one white and vaulted with a thick, rustic beam down its center. A cool breeze caressed my face, diluting the sweet floral with air that smelled of rain and earth.

Definitely not Los Angeles.

"You're awake," said the Omega.

I turned my head on the pillow, blinking groggily. "Déjà vu."

Adam looked every inch an All-American college boy in jeans and a dark, hooded sweatshirt. His eyes, however, showed his age, and more than that, his deep fatigue. Thinking of the needle he'd stabbed me in the arm with, I hoped he was tired because of me.

"How are you feeling, Fiona?"

I sat up carefully but to my surprise, I felt fine, if hungry and weak. "Okay, I guess."

The newest bedroom in my twisted game of musical beds was by far the largest. Done in tones of pale blue, dove gray, and white, it was hands down the most beautiful living space I'd ever seen, and easily the square footage of my entire apartment.

Before an elegant stone fireplace was a cozy seating area that begged for lazy afternoons reading and drinking tea. Plush cream rugs were strewn in intervals over dark, rustic wood floors, and huge bay windows displayed a dim, overcast sky with a canopy of green forest in the distance.

"Is it morning or evening?" I asked, turning back to the Omega.

"Evening," he said haltingly.

Now fully awake, my mind churned. "Is it still Saturday?"

"No, Sunday."

Which meant I'd been unconscious for the better part of two days.

"Wow," I whispered, pressing the heels of my hands into my eyes to subdue a sudden urge to cry. Or scream. Potentially both. But since neither was an option, I used the classic standby, "I need to use the bathroom."

Adam stood immediately and gestured to an open doorway not far from the bed. "Of course. It's through there. You'll find the bag your uncle packed for you inside."

"Thanks," I muttered.

"You might feel a little light-headed, perhaps experience some blurred vision. It will fade as your body acclimates to my spell, but you should take it easy for a few hours."

I swallowed the sudden pulse in my throat. At the sight of my face, Adam's eyes narrowed.

"Your uncle didn't tell you?"

"Tell me what?"

His gaze flickered to my arms, and mine followed. At first, I didn't see anything amiss. Glistening, narrow ribbons of scarring—Check. Then it hit me. No longer did black script obscure the scars. Mal's spells were gone. Instead, encircling my wrists were delicate woven bracelets. Tight enough to not slip off, and with no visible catches for removal. One was white, the other black.

Breathing a little faster, I lifted my hands and clenched them. Nothing. No electricity at all.

"The bracelets are positive and negative," said the Omega. "To equalize your charge."

I took a deep, slow breath. Logically, I should be relieved, even grateful. *Shouldn't I be grateful?* It was extraordinary magic, a true testament to Adam's skill.

But I wasn't relieved. I felt like the most vital piece of me had been sawed off, the wound cauterized.

"You neutered me," I said through numb lips.

"For your protection," he countered firmly.

I touched the bracelet on my left wrist, the black one, then looked up at him. I was suddenly, immensely angry.

"Don't you mean *his* protection?"

Adam stared at me for a considering beat, then nodded sharply. Gone was the unassuming youth— here was the Opal Mage. Sparkling power formed a pale corona around his shoulders and head. The sight of it was actually comforting; at least I hadn't lost the ability to see magic.

"I don't know you, Fiona Sullivan," he said flatly. "You have a tremendous and dangerous power, and very little discipline. Must I remind you that in a fit of temper you threw a lightning bolt at the Western Prime?"

I bristled further, teeth clenching around the words, "I only did what he wanted! And what about him? He almost bit me. You want to tell me that was part of the test?"

Brown irises bled to white and I recoiled against

the headboard. "That is exactly the problem," he said darkly. "The Prime has not drunk from a human vein in more than a hundred years. Because of you, he nearly broke his most sacred vow."

I almost bit my tongue in half. "Wait—he was going to bite me for real? Not in a dream but in real life?"

"Yes," he snapped. "And I wouldn't have been able to stop him. You have zero understanding of your own power. Are you even aware of the physics of a lightning strike? The massive particle disruption that occurs prior to and because of it?"

A soft voice spoke from the doorway, "Leave her be, Adam."

The Omega glared at me another moment, grunted in disgust, then stalked across the room. He brushed past the Prime like the vampire, too, was intolerable.

"Don't take his words too much to heart. He's worried."

I looked anywhere but at the man leaning in the doorway. Possibly the oldest vamp in the world, who'd almost broken a century-long fast on my jugular.

"It's not a fast so much as a test of endurance."

I shook my head helplessly. "How do you sound so amused? This isn't funny. Any of it."

"No, it's not," said the Prime in a grave tone, for once devoid of humor. "I would like to try teaching you discipline, Fiona, if you'll let me."

I said nothing, overwhelmed by the way my life had been upended, and still reeling from the back-to-back confrontations. First with the Prime in the Colosseum, and now with the Omega.

Two of the scariest fuckers out there.

Curling into myself, I lifted my knees and hugged them to my chest. I wasn't too proud to admit I was a million miles outside my comfort zone. I was scared, worried about my dad and Mal, and still partly convinced I was going to end up in a mad scientist's laboratory. And without my lightning I was now a null, completely at the mercy of supernaturals.

The Prime took a step into the bedroom. "I promised your uncle I would keep you safe, and I will."

"Stop reading my mind," I whispered. "Please, stop. I can't take it anymore."

The events of the last forty-eight hours hit like a freight train, the impact forcing a whimper from my chest. I'd been cut up, slammed into a wall, almost bitten, bespelled, drugged, threatened, and power-neutered.

And my dad was missing. Maybe hurt, or worse.

I was helpless to stop the first strangled sob, or the second. All at once the floodgates opened, and I was crying in front of the Western Prime. Not a contained, feminine sniffling, either. No—I was slave to a full-blown, horrendously loud sob-fest.

When arms came around me, lifted me, and settled me against a solid chest, I was too far gone to care who they belonged to. It had been so long since I'd been held. So damned long.

"Hush, *mo spréach*. All will be well. I will keep you safe."

Against my better judgement, I believed him.

6

REALITY CRASHED MY PITY-PARTY FAST. **Before** the Prime's shirt could absorb more than a few of my tears, I jumped from his arms and raced into the bathroom. Locking the door behind me, I cranked on the water in a massive, glass-enclosed shower, tore off my smelly clothes, and inserted myself into the scalding flow.

I let the water rinse the final tears from my face, breathing in short bursts until the wall around my emotions was rebuilt—a familiar exercise that didn't take long.

Growing up with a single male parent, a police detective to boot, hadn't afforded me much leeway for feminine hysterics. From a young age, I'd recognized the deep sadness my stalwart father concealed and modified my behavior accordingly.

The older I grew, the more my role evolved. As soon as I arrived home from school, I started cooking a healthy dinner for the two of us. I did the laundry, cleaned the house, and made sure his favorite magazines were stocked beside his recliner. I was too busy for teenaged tantrums, moping, or lovesickness. By self-appointment, I was his rock.

When the time arrived for me to fill out college applications, my dad had expressly forbidden me from applying to schools in Los Angeles. I'd been shocked by the pronouncement. Hurt and betrayed. He'd decided he didn't need me anymore—didn't want me anymore.

It took a few years for me to understand that, in his stoic way, he'd given me a gift. I'd gone north to Berkeley and had the best four years of my life. The most important lesson I'd learned was that sometimes the greatest act of love was letting someone go.

God, I really hoped he was okay.

It had been a long time since I'd showered minus sparks. So long that at first, the lack of electricity was disconcerting. Eventually, though, I resigned myself to somatic pleasure. I'd never experienced a waterfall showerhead before.

When my skin was red and puckered, I turned my attention to the row of bath products displayed on a cutout shelf. I scrubbed my body until it was raw, shaved my legs, and washed and conditioned my hair until it was a silky sheet down my back. When there was nothing else to do except wait for the water to go cold, I regretfully turned off the flow.

The largest, fluffiest towels I'd ever seen waited on a heated rack. I wrapped one around my head and the other around my body, then unzipped the overnight bag left by the door.

"Jesus, Mal," I muttered as I pulled out the third sports bra.

Clearly, my uncle hadn't been able to bring himself to open my actual underwear drawer, as there were no panties or regular bras. There were two tank tops, two pairs of leggings I ran in, and three long-sleeved shirts. Tennis shoes but no socks. A pair of flip-flops. No jacket or sweatshirt for the cooler climate. At least he'd packed deodorant, though that was the limit of personal hygiene products.

Thanks a bunch, Mal.

I settled on black leggings and a long-sleeved black shirt. The color suited my frame of mind. Dark and determined.

Sometime between shaving my legs and conditioning my hair, I'd come to a conclusion. I wanted my lightning back. As far as I saw it, the only way that was going to happen was if I let the Prime teach me discipline. Whatever that entailed. I wasn't convinced he could or that it was even possible, but after weighing my options, it was the only chance I had of getting what I wanted.

For starters, my life back.

By the time I finished dressing, I had barely enough energy to towel-dry my hair. Two days in a magical coma probably had something to do with it; either that, or I was experiencing the side effects Adam had mentioned.

Slipping my feet into flip-flops, I unlocked the bathroom door and peeked out, immediately heaving a sigh of relief at the sight of an empty room. No alluring, mind-reading vamps or white-eyed mages in the vicinity.

Every step toward the closed bedroom door ratcheted up my anxiety. From a quick survey out the windows at a heavily forested, twilit terrain, I was relatively certain I was at the Prime's compound outside Seattle. If so, and if the gossip rags were correct, I was surrounded by not only vamps and mages, but the third spoke of the Prime's triumvirate, the Alpha, and his pack of werewolves.

I considered crawling back into bed and waiting for someone to make sure I was still alive, but gnawing hunger pains won out.

With a deep breath for courage, I swung open the bedroom door and abruptly loosed an undignified yelp. An unfamiliar, scowling man stood directly opposite me, his fist raised to knock. He was built like a lumberjack, with unkempt dark hair, a trimmed beard, and piercing, pale blue eyes. Power leaked from him in a continuous stream, thick and pulsing like a heartbeat.

Icy eyes surveyed me from head to toe, stalling a few moments on my messy, wet hair before settling on my face. The scowl never faltered as he growled, "I'm Declan."

Declan Thomas, the Western Alpha.

I sighed. "I really can't catch a break, can I?"

To my everlasting shock, the scowl melted from Declan's features. A wide grin looked much more at home on his face. It also radically altered my first impression of him, as well as his overall attractiveness.

I stuck out my hand, figuring I might as well take advantage of being able to touch people. "I'm Fiona Sullivan. Nice to meet you."

He looked at my hand, then glanced up with a wicked glint in his eye. "I bet you're hell at parties."

I wrinkled my nose. "What?"

He pointed at my hand, which was still hanging

in the air but beginning to wilt. "You know, zapping unsuspecting people."

Great, another jackass.

I sighed and let my hand fall, but Declan caught it before it reached my side, giving it a firm shake before releasing me. A marked ruddiness stained his cheekbones.

"I'm sorry, that was in poor taste. Good to meet you, Fiona." He cleared his throat. "I was told you might be hungry."

"God, yes," I said emphatically.

Declan chuckled. "I can fix that. Follow me."

We walked down an elegant hallway with dark wood floors and white walls to the elevator at its end. Declan depressed a button on the wall, then pulled a keycard from his pocket.

"I'd better give this to you now so I don't forget," he said and handed it to me.

I stared dubiously at the silver card, not plastic as I'd assumed, but a lightweight metal etched with a complex design.

"What's this for?"

"The elevator. Access to this floor is restricted."

I glanced back down the hallway. Across from the bedroom I'd woken up in was another, matching door, and at the far end were double doors. All were closed. A touch of claustrophobia tickled the back of my throat.

I looked at Declan. "A key to my own prison, huh?"

He squinted at me in confusion. "You're a guest, not a prisoner." At my skeptical look, he continued intently, "You're staying in the private residence of the Prime. His rooms are at the end of the hall and the one opposite yours is his library."

I blinked, shook my head, and blinked again, but the words were still ridiculous. Declan smirked. "Most women would kill to be in your position, but from the look on your face, I'd say you'd rather run screaming."

I blurted, "What if the elevator breaks?"

He frowned. "Why would it break?"

I opened my mouth, then closed it, realizing my former issues with disrupting electrical circuits were, at least temporarily, irrelevant.

"Are there stairs, at least?"

Declan's pale eyes twinkled with humor. "Hatching an escape plan?"

In spite of my anxiety, I grinned. "I thought you said I wasn't a prisoner."

The elevator pinged and the doors parted on a willowy blond. At the sight of us, she paused mid-step, her full red lips parting in surprise. Hazel eyes narrowed on Declan before shifting to my face. I winced at the cold *zing* of eye contact and looked quickly down.

I wasn't sure if she was a daywalker vamp like the Prime or had been turned by Ascension, but either way, she was packing a lot of power. And I was defenseless.

"Who is this?" she snapped. "Where's Connor?"

Declan stood stiffly beside me, clearly not a fan of the vamp. Based on the disdain I'd glimpsed in my brief eye contact with her, I felt safe predicting I wasn't going to be a fan, either.

"Samantha, this is Fiona."

I glanced at Declan sharply—his voice was a bit too smug for comfort. My suspicions were confirmed when he added brightly, "She's staying in the Consort's suite."

The resulting silence was almost worse than hysterics. Still avoiding eye contact with the vamp, I shifted until Declan's broad shoulder was between us. If she came at me, I wanted him in the way.

Behind us, a door clicked open.

"Samantha," said that smooth, amused voice I was beginning to loathe. "Ms. Sullivan is immune to you, so you may cease trying to influence her."

I stiffened in surprise, glancing over my shoulder to see a bare-chested Prime standing in the library's doorway. Unsurprisingly, his upper body was a study in chiseled perfection.

My mouth went a little dry.

"Declan, please don't bait Samantha. And Fiona…" His gaze flickered to my hair. "After you've eaten, please join me in the library."

When he looked at Samantha and nodded once, I started breathing again. She strode past us, graceful on her four-inch stilettos, but not before sliding me a glare of undiluted malice. I instinctively recoiled, which brought me flush to Declan's side. His shifter aura was a good deal more potent than my father's, but was familiar enough to dull the edges of my fear.

"You okay?" he murmured.

I shuddered. "Yeah. She's a real peach."

He snorted, and we watched like voyeurs of a train wreck as Samantha greeted the Prime with a full-body press and an excess of tongue.

"Yuck," I breathed, shaking my head. "Can we go?"

"Hell yes," said Declan, and we stepped quickly into the elevator.

The doors began to slide shut, and because I couldn't help myself, I took one more look down the hallway. Samantha's mouth was on the Prime's throat, her blond head tucked into his neck. His eyes, now dark as the forest outside, were locked on mine.

When the elevator doors thumped closed, I released a shaky breath and glanced at Declan. "Let me guess, Samantha's the jealous type?"

He smirked. "You could say that. I'm sure after Connor explains your presence, she'll leave you alone."

I sighed, doubting his assessment. "Is there a private kitchen? I don't think I can handle any more surprises tonight."

He nodded, eyes softening with compassion. "Adam told me why you're here, and about the spelled bracelets. I can't begin to imagine what you must be feeling right now. If someone took away my ability to shift..." He shook his head, whistling beneath his breath.

I clenched my hands, his words compounding my ache of loss. "It's not pleasant, I'll say that."

"I'm sure it's only temporary."

He didn't sound convinced, and neither did I as I said, "Yeah, temporary."

7

DECLAN THOMAS MADE a mean grilled cheese sandwich, packed with basil, tomatoes, and four types of cheese. After I scarfed down two of them, he insisted I drink two tall glasses of water to rehydrate. In reward, he presented me with an icy bottle of imported beer.

We sat at a table in a small kitchen somewhere in the rear of the Prime's compound. The main kitchen, he explained, would be chaos at this hour, filling dinner orders for hundreds of shifters and mages, and bottled breakfasts for newly risen vamps. As promised, he'd circumvented the main hallways by sticking to stairwells and shadowed corridors. Whether intentional or not, I had no hope of finding my way back to the elevator without him.

I eventually found the courage to ask him why

he'd been scowling when I opened the door. He told me he'd been thinking about his laundry. After having a good laugh, we did the usual small talk routine. Favorite sports teams. Starbucks or Seattle's Best. Star Trek or Star Wars, et cetera. The conversation veered off, evolved, and I soon concluded that at least one member of the Western Triumvirate was relatively normal.

After accepting my second beer, I asked, "So tell me, is it a big, happy, cross-species family here at the compound?"

Declan took a swig from his own bottle before replying. "Hardly, but interaction is mostly limited to meal times and weekly assemblies. It helps that Connor built three separate wings with private entrances and exits. The two above ground are for the shifters and mages, the one below for the vamps."

I whistled. "I can understand you having your pack close, but why so many vamps and mages?"

He gave me a look that said he wholeheartedly agreed, but capitulated with, "The mages are here to learn from the Omega. There's usually twenty or so living onsite at any given time. As for the vamps, it's not a well-known fact, but Connor maintained a nest after being appointed Prime. He has thirty vamps who call him master."

I shuddered in exaggerated horror. "Including Samantha, I presume?"

Declan shook his head, grinning. "He met her at a benefit function in Seattle last year. She definitely wants to be invited into the fold, though. In case you didn't notice, she has her eye on that Consort's suite."

I thought of Samantha as I'd last seen her, her face against the Prime's neck. Grimacing, I asked, "Does he feed all his vamps?"

He nodded, humored by my reaction. "Some more than others. It's considered a great gift to drink from one as old as he." I lifted my brows questioningly and he grinned. "Oh, no. You'll have to ask him yourself."

I brought my beer to my lips, only to realize the bottle was empty. The heady brew had warmed my muscles and given me a pleasant glow.

I set the bottle down and sighed. "I suppose it's time to answer the Prime's summons."

"You don't have to call him that," said Declan with mirth. "He prefers Connor."

I shook my head but didn't elaborate. I wasn't sure I could. Connor Thorne was the Prime, nothing more or less. Instead, I stood and clasped my hands before my chest.

"Take me to your leader?"

He laughed, standing to collect our bottles and toss them into a nearby recycle bin. He met me at the entrance to the kitchen. "You, Fiona Sullivan, are an interesting woman. I'm not sure there's many people who, in your position, would be joking around."

I winked, aware that the booze had made me flirty but unable to put a cap on it. "I have a high tolerance for crazy."

Declan grinned, reaching up to touch the hair beside my temple. It was a light touch, but I felt it to my toes.

"Have you ever tried to dye this?"

"Oh, yes, with every dye known to man. It won't take color. At least it's small enough I can hide it under the rest of my hair."

He gave me an odd look. "You can't hide this." His large, warm hand stroked across the side of my head. "It's the width of my palm."

A peculiar sensation tingled across the back of my neck. "What? No, it's not."

I reached up and our hands connected. Declan stilled, his pale eyes taking on a yellow tinge. Abruptly, he pulled away and took a step back, turning toward the door.

"Come on," he said gruffly. "Let's get you back."

I followed him meekly, barely paying attention to

my surroundings except to look for a mirror. I saw no reason for Declan to lie, but still struggled to make sense of it. If what he said was true, then sometime during the last forty-eight hours, the inch-thick streak of white in my hair had quadrupled.

By the time we reached the familiar hallway of the Prime's residence, I hadn't seen a mirror, but had a pretty good idea of when the change had happened.

When I stepped from the elevator, Declan didn't follow. "I'll leave you here," he said, giving me a jaunty salute. "Good luck."

Gratitude flooded me, along with a surprisingly potent affection given we'd just met. The feeling, I knew, was more than just a result of the beer in my belly. Our impromptu meal and conversation had been marked with an ease of companionship I hadn't felt since before Ascension. He'd touched me, too, but unlike the Prime, he was warm, engaging, and relatable.

Before I could rein in the impulse, I asked, "Dinner tomorrow?"

Surprise flared in his eyes, quickly replaced by pleasure. "Absolutely. Have a good night, Fiona."

I was still staring at the closed elevator doors when, from somewhere behind me, a low voice said, "Before you launch into dangerous territory, I should warn you that Declan is romantically involved with a shifter in his pack."

My beer buzz vanished in a flash. I turned, meeting the gaze of the Prime. He leaned against the library doorjamb, dressed casually in black lounge pants and a white T-shirt that stretched across his broad shoulders. Muscled arms were crossed over his chest; he looked like he'd been watching me awhile.

I stuffed down my embarrassment. "I asked you to stop reading my mind."

"I didn't. There was lift in your core body temperature and the release of pheromones. I smelled the direction of your thoughts."

I blinked. "That's disturbing. And invasive."

"I agree," he said mildly. "I would prefer not to smell you at all. Your odor is exceedingly distracting."

Heat bloomed in my cheeks and I stifled the urge to sniff my armpit. I couldn't remember if I'd used the deodorant Mal had packed.

Gritting my teeth, I said, "It's not my fault you don't like the shampoo left in the shower."

His full lips thinned. "That's not what I meant."

This man was going to make me pull my hair out by the roots. "What did you mean, then?" I growled.

His eyes flashed dark. "You smell unlike any

human I've ever met. I can only speculate it's due to your Ascension."

Huh. I hadn't been expecting that.

I wasn't sure I wanted to know the answer, but still asked, "What do I smell like?"

His nostrils flared and his eyes darkened even further. I didn't realize I'd moved backward until my spine connected with the elevator doors.

"Like a summer thunderstorm," he murmured, then shook his head sharply. The darkness in his eyes fled, revealing the familiar wry, leafy green depths. "Come into the library, please. There's someone I would have you meet."

As he turned, I said, "Wait," and when he faced me, I pointed at the side of my head. "Were you going to mention this?"

His brows rose. "I assumed the mirror in the bathroom was mention enough."

"It was fogged up." I made my feet carry me toward him. "It happened because of the lightning bolt, didn't it? You probably know that was a first for me."

He nodded. "That was my conclusion, yes."

The closer I moved to him, the more imposing he became. Taller than Declan, though more slender, everything about his lithe build screamed *predator.* Somehow, too, he was even scarier in casual garb than in a suit. I no longer wanted to see him in a gladiator costume—I'd probably faint.

The memory of his bare chest flashed in my mind and I forcefully countered the thought with one from the Colosseum: black eyes and fangs intent on biting me.

I stopped several feet from him and gazed into his eyes. A dangerous risk, but necessary. My dad had taught me that when you met someone who scared you, sometimes the only defense was a bluff. The Prime needed to know I wasn't afraid of him. Or at the least, that my fear of him couldn't control me.

His eyes remained neutral green, his expression aloof. I frowned at him. "Why am I immune to Samantha's power but not yours?"

When Connor Thorne smiled fully, I wouldn't be surprised to find out the world tilted a little on its axis. A dimple appeared in his left cheek and small, charming creases fanned from the corners of his eyes. I'll admit, I was a little dumbstruck. And though I might wish to blame it on his vamp glamour, the truth was more primal. He was, quite simply, the most attractive man I'd ever seen.

"I'm somewhat unique," he replied blithely.

I pulled together my scattered wits. "Is that why I can't sense your aura?" The sucking void of his power, that I'd felt in my dad's office in L.A., had been absent in our interactions since.

His smile softened. "No. You can't sense it because I choose for you not to. Your sensitivity to auras and your ability to see magic are highly unusual qualities. Whether they're linked to your Ascension or predate it remains to be seen. Regardless, your lack of sufficient defenses makes these abilities problematic in my presence."

"I didn't sense auras before Ascension," I countered, then frowned. "Wait, are you saying your power is so great you'd fry my brain?"

All traces of humor vanished from his face and eyes. "That's exactly what I'm saying." He gestured to the doorway. "Come inside. We've kept our guest waiting long enough."

I bit my tongue and walked past him, straight into a book lover's dream. Every wall except the one boasting high, paned windows was covered in dark shelving. A combination of recessed and modern pendant lighting illumined hundreds of tightly packed books, richly woven rugs, distressed leather couches, and an eclectic assortment of cushioned chairs.

From a chair near the windows rose a slim, gray-haired woman. She was eighty if she was a day, and garbed in familiar white robes. Her face was heavily lined, but with the kind of wrinkles that bespoke a life well lived rather than too much time in the sun.

"The fifth Opal," I said, mostly to myself.

Lively dark eyes scanned my face. "Fiona Sullivan," she said in a clear voice. "You look just like your mother. I'm curious, were your eyes blue like hers before Ascension, or have they always been gray?"

The breath in my lungs stilled. My heartbeat drummed a staccato rhythm in my ears.

"What did you say?" I whispered.

The Prime touched my arm, I think maybe to comfort me, but I jerked away, hissing, "Don't touch me."

The Opal glanced curiously between us. Whatever she saw on the Prime's face seemed to amuse her. The slight smile fell, however, when she looked at me again.

"I can see I've shocked you, which was not my intention. Will you sit and allow me to explain why I'm here?"

My muscles remained locked. "If it has anything to do with my mother, I'm not interested."

She nodded. "I will not speak of Delilah."

Delilah.

Gah, I hated that name.

The Opal settled back into her seat. I took the

one opposite hers, while across the room, the Prime dropped onto one of the couches. He swung his legs onto the adjacent cushions and folded his arms behind his head, settling back to watch us with an avid gaze.

I returned the mage's scrutiny with a glare, as mention of my mother turned me into a raging antagonist.

"You know me, but I don't know you."

My companion merely smiled. "My name is Alisande Salvator. Yes, I'm an Opal Mage, though I was one long before Ascension changed the world. Back then, I was called a witch." She glanced briefly at the Prime. "I'd like to perceive your magic, if you'll allow it."

I shifted, the words pinging discordantly. "I don't have any magic."

"Ah," she said, like it was a revelation. My scalp tingled unpleasantly. I blamed the pale corona of power crackling around her. "Perhaps magic isn't the most accurate term. Your sensitivity to auras and magical resonance, then."

Instinctively, I looked at the Prime. He was watching me, one eyebrow lifted, lightly mocking and blatantly challenging. His earlier words occupied the space between us: *I will keep you safe.*

Did I trust him? Not as far as I could throw him.

But on the other hand, he hadn't given me any reason to doubt his word. Yet.

"Okay."

Alisande's smile widened as she came to her feet. She was a tiny woman—even with me sitting, she was barely taller than me. Delicate hands lifted and I flinched.

"It won't hurt," she murmured.

Soft fingers came to rest on either side of my face. My vision tunneled and went dark.

8

I OPENED MY EYES, assessed that I was alive and lying supine on a couch in the library, and closed them again.

"I'm getting sick of this."

The Prime's low chuckle sounded from across the room. "And I grow tired of carting your unconscious body to the nearest flat surface."

I sighed and dropped a forearm over my face. "Is she gone?"

"Yes," he said, much closer now. I peered from beneath my arm to see him standing over me. He frowned, opened his mouth to speak, then seemed to think better of it.

"What?" I pressed, lifting my arm.

"Before we discuss what she learned, I thought you should know I heard from Malcolm."

I sat up so fast my head spun. "Did he find my dad?"

"Not yet, though he has a promising lead."

"What is it?"

The Prime strode across the room to a small cabinet. "Would you like a brandy?"

I considered tossing a couch cushion at his back, and almost did as he threw his head back and laughed. The warm, infectious sound almost distracted me from his violation.

"Get out of my head!"

He faced me, his eyes still crinkled merrily at the corners. "*Mo spréach*, you throw your thoughts like you do lightning."

Mo spréach.

I remembered him calling me that once before. It sounded Gaelic, but although my dad and Malcolm's parents were Irish transplants to the U.S., the language had passed from the family generations ago.

No way in hell was I going to give the Prime the satisfaction of asking what it meant. From his tone, it was either an endearment or a demeaning moniker. Both options set my teeth on edge.

"Brandy?" he asked again, lifting a glass tumbler in my direction.

I nodded shortly, and moments later was

presented with two fingers of liquor. He tossed back his own serving before settling at the far end of the couch. I lifted my glass and took a healthy swallow, the fiery elixir burning my throat and clearing my head.

"Does this mean Mal is coming to Seattle?"

The Prime nodded. "He'll be here tomorrow afternoon."

I took another sip of brandy, staring at his profile over the rim of my glass. "What do you think happened to my dad? I'm assuming it has something to do with the case he was working for you."

"I would agree."

"You didn't answer my question."

He glanced at me, brows raised. "I don't make a habit of sharing case details with laypersons. Nor do I think your father would approve of me sharing these particular details."

I swallowed hard. "Tell me this much: do you think he's dead?"

He was silent long enough that I knew the next words he spoke would be bullshit.

His lips curved wryly. "I'm damned either way with you, aren't I?"

I shook my head. "You don't understand. My dad and Mal are the only family I have. The people who accepted and protected me the last fourteen years." I rubbed the aching space over my heart. "I'm not an innocent, either, if you're thinking to spare me horror. I grew up with a cop for a father. I've even helped on cases in recent years when he's needed to track mages. I'm not asking for the gory details, Connor. Just give me something. Anything to hold onto."

A small, weighted pause ensued. "So you do know my name."

I flushed and quickly swallowed the last of the brandy, then set the glass on a side table. Standing, I narrowed my eyes on the side of his expressionless face. "Since I was unconscious for the last two days, I doubt I'll be sleeping tonight. Can I borrow a book?"

His lashes dropped, shadowing his eyes. "Sit down."

"No."

He sighed. "A group of ciphers calling themselves the Liberati are capturing and torturing supernaturals. Experimenting on them. They've been extremely circumspect with their victims until recently, when a shifter escaped confinement and managed to share his story before dying from his wounds."

I sat back down, my mind reeling. "Isn't this FBI territory? How does my father come into this?"

"The FBI is investigating, but so am I. I asked for Frank's help because of you."

"I'm sorry, what?" I choked out.

He finally looked at me, gaze steady and unapologetic. "The Prime's Office has been aware of you for a long time. Your first registration with Census, when you received a cipher classification, was a ruse. We've been watching you, waiting to see how your powers would manifest."

I shook my head slowly. "I don't understand."

"Forgive my bluntness, but my goal is to use you. I need your skills to track the ciphers responsible for more than sixty suspected murders nationwide. You said it yourself: you've worked with your father tracking mages. My hope, in contacting Frank, was that he would enlist your help. I underestimated a parent's drive to protect his child." He sighed lightly. "Had you been more patient, all this would have been revealed tomorrow."

"I'm not..." I knuckled my eyes. "You're wrong. I didn't sense anything at my dad's office."

"I know. Malcolm's spells helped you manage your lightning, but they also dampened your ability to perceive magical resonance. Resonance is an echo of a person's aura, like a fingerprint. The stronger the aura, the longer its resonance stays in a place and the more easily you can sense it. For example, have you ever entered a room after your uncle left it and felt like he was still there?" Interpreting my scowl of annoyance as confirmation, he continued, "What you sensed was Malcolm's personal resonance. In time, you'll learn how to differentiate between different species and people, just like a wolf can catalogue and track thousands of scents."

The patient, measured tone of his voice made me want to scratch my eyes out. I said irritably, "Thanks for the refresher, but none of that is news to me. I'm telling you, there wasn't any resonance at the office."

"But there was," he countered with insufferable calm. "Alchemy is magic. It's merely a different kind, one you haven't learned to perceive. Alchemists don't harness power from within, as mages do, but use a catalyst to activate spells. In the last decade, the art, so to speak, has quickly advanced. Practicing cipher alchemists have discovered that the most effective catalyst is derived from the blood of supernaturals."

I pinched the bridge of my nose. "Why haven't I heard anything about this? I don't watch the news every day or anything, but this is pretty huge."

"No comment."

My breath expelled in a huff. "Figured you'd say that." I tried another angle. "Didn't both my uncle and Adam sense the alchemy at the office? If mages can sense it, what do you need me for?"

"For mages, alchemy is akin to a general sense of wrongness. There are no distinguishing features. So although they can recognize it, they can't track it. You can. And you will."

Anxiety tightened around my chest like a vise. The walls seemed to waver and move closer, igniting claustrophobia. I jerked to my feet and paced across the room.

"I thought it would be because of my lightning."

"What would?" he asked, in a tone that said he already knew the answer.

"I always knew someone would find me. Abduct me." My voice rose with every word, edged with hysteria. "To use me. Survival of the fittest, right? But I'm not a predator. Not like you. I never had a chance!"

"Fiona."

I spun, jabbing a finger in his direction. "All your fancy words and 'I'll protect you' bullshit can quit. I don't want to hear anything else. I just want to go home!"

Every muscle in my body quivered like I'd just completed a fifty-yard dash. My chest heaved, my breath rasping in the sudden silence. The Prime sat completely still, his lips slightly parted, his pupils pinpricks amidst the muted green glow of his eyes.

Instinct screamed at me to run, but it warred with an equally potent, nearly magnetic compulsion to go to him. To fall at his feet. Obey him.

"Unbelievable. You're mind-fucking me without even trying, aren't you?"

He blinked, releasing a slow breath. "You need to leave," he said in a low, chilling voice. "Go. Right now."

I laughed shrilly. "Really? Should I bow, too? Or maybe curtsy? What does Samantha do when you order her around?"

I was quite possibly the stupidest person on the planet.

Cool fingers surrounded my throat in a deceptively gentle grip. I hadn't seen him move. Not even a blur. I think my heart stopped for a few seconds before resuming its beat with a roar.

The Prime tilted my head back, angling my face to his. His eyes were still green—thank God—but I could clearly see fangs behind his lips. They looked decidedly sharp, the tips so fine they were almost invisible.

"Never, in more than a millennia, have I met a creature as irreverent as you," he murmured silkily. His thumbs pressed deeply into either side of my throat, cutting off blood flow until my vision dimmed. "So fragile." His fingers gentled, stroking lightly. "And yet so resilient. Alisande seems to think you're worth the incredible risk I'm taking on you."

"Not… worth it," I wheezed.

The library door slammed open and I glimpsed Adam, white-eyed and ready to rock.

"Connor, what the fuck? Are you all right?"

The Prime ignored him, continuing his sensual torture on my throat, thumbs sliding up to my jaw and down to my collarbone in teasing, circular patterns. Letting me feel his strength, his dominance.

I cursed him even as I felt arousal surge, hot and heavy in my blood. His nostrils flared and—if I wasn't hallucinating—his fangs extended further.

"Don't let it go to your head," I ground out. "I've had a fourteen-year drought."

His lips twitched, involuntarily it seemed, then parted in a grin. A short chuckle escaped him, then another, until he was laughing uproariously. Stumbling backward, he collapsed on a nearby couch and covered his face with his hands. From the noises he was making, he'd just heard the best joke of his life.

Drunk on adrenaline and the sound of the

Prime's laughter, I glanced across the room at Adam. "I think I broke him."

He stared at me for a long moment, some feeling I couldn't name in his eyes. If I didn't know better, I'd say it was admiration.

"Maybe you should head to your room, Fiona."

I nodded. "Excellent idea."

I snagged a couple of books on my way out.

9

THE MORNING DAWNED clear and bright, with birds chirping and breezes blowing. From a window in my pretty prison, I watched six large and beautiful wolves streak from the compound toward the forest. I envied them. Even hated them, a little.

I was in a mood.

Upon returning to my room the previous night, I'd spent the better part of six excruciating hours twiddling my thumbs. I'd rearranged the furniture before the fireplace, thumbed through two extremely dry tomes on European history, and unpacked my meager belongings into a dresser. I'd even searched every pocket of my overnight bag twice, in case I missed something Mal had snuck in for me. A cell phone. A pack of gum. Even a deck of cards would have been welcome.

Sleep finally claimed me a few hours before dawn, only to abandon me at the first touch of light in the sky. After another marathon shower, I'd spent an inordinate amount of time staring at myself in the mirror.

You look just like your mother.

Maybe I did. I wouldn't know, as she'd left just after my birth and my father hadn't kept any pictures of her. At a young age, I'd been sworn to silence on the subject, though Mal had given me a few nuggets over the years.

She'd been beautiful and troubled. Charming and selfish. Emotionally volatile. Before her marriage to my father, Delilah Greer had been a self-professed bohemian, never staying in one city long. Mal had told me that when she'd been pregnant with me, she'd sometimes disappeared for days at a time.

But despite her varied and hurtful idiosyncrasies, my father had been nuts about her. When she'd left him with a newborn and no word, he'd been inconsolable. If it hadn't been for Mal, and eventually me, he might have gone off the deep end.

Once, I'd come home from college on a surprise visit. When I'd let myself into the house, I'd found my dad drunk in his recliner. Misled by booze and darkness, he'd mistaken me for my long lost mother. My strong, proud father had cried out and fallen to his knees. The following day, it was understood we would never mention the incident.

Outside, leaves swirled across a courtyard of gray stone. The shadows of wolves darted inside the forest line.

I decided to go for a run.

Not giving myself time for second thoughts, I stuffed my feet in sneakers, grabbed the metal keycard from the dresser, and headed out the door. The hallway was silent and empty. As I waited for the elevator, I ignored the itch between my shoulder blades, as well as the impulse to glance behind me every few seconds.

The paneled doors opened without incident. I hurried inside, jabbing the button for the ground floor while glancing periodically down the hall. By the time the elevator started moving, my heart was pounding.

When the doors opened again, I was almost relieved to see Adam's familiar face. He blinked in surprise. "Where are you going?"

I squared my shoulders. "For a run."

He took in my sockless, sneakered feet. "Uh-huh."

Behind him was what looked like the lobby of an expensive hotel. Lofty ceiling, navy walls, glassy, dark wood floors, and elaborate crown molding. An immense, intricate chandelier dominated the central space, hundreds of glimmering crystal strands dripping downward like frozen rain. Artwork hung in intervals along the walls, bold and impressionistic, massive pieces like those you saw in museums but never in private homes. Corridors with arched entries lined both sides of the hall, branching off to God only knew where.

And there were people. A lot of them. Milling around, crossing to and from adjacent hallways. A good number were currently staring at me.

My expression wasn't as controlled as I thought, because Adam sighed and said, "Come with me. I'll show you the trailhead."

I tried to take a deep breath, but it stuck in my throat. "Thanks," I croaked, but he'd already turned away and was striding toward a set of gargantuan wooden doors. They were, of course, on the far side of the lobby, and reaching them was going to be the equivalent of walking through a minefield of auras.

Sure enough, by the time I caught up with Adam, I was twitching. *Fiona Sullivan, Supernatural Punching Bag.* Maybe I should have business cards made up.

There were a few daywalker vamps and at least fifteen shifters, and while their auras were invasive, those radiating from the dozen or so mages were plain unsettling. The Ruby, Amber, and Topaz Mages weren't so bad, but there were seven Emerald and three Sapphire. None of them were bothering to dampen their coronas, as Adam and Mal did.

I'd never taken LSD, but could imagine the effect was something like what I was seeing.

Maybe the repression of my lightning had enhanced my sensitivity, or Mal's spells had been protecting me more than I'd thought, but I was seriously out of my depth.

By chance, I glanced aside as we passed another archway. Standing beside a familiar, poster-perfect blonde was the Prime. Samantha was glaring at me, while the Prime watched me with half-lidded eyes. His lips curved as I caught his gaze. He gave me a short nod, then returned his attention to his crazy girlfriend.

"Fiona!"

I looked around and saw Declan striding toward us. At the sight of his smiling face, a knot inside me loosened. The closer he came, the more relaxed I felt, until I was virtually purring in his warm, pulsing energy. Just ahead of me, Adam stopped and turned, nodding a greeting to the Alpha.

Declan returned the nod, then grinned down at me. "Where are you off to?"

I returned his smile. "I thought I'd go for a run. You know, plot my escape."

He laughed and glanced skeptically at my feet. "Without socks?"

I shrugged. "I've done it before."

He nodded perfunctorily. "I had you pegged for a runner."

My brows went up—he might as well have said *nice legs*. Declan seemed to arrive at the same conclusion and blushed, which only made me smile wider.

He glanced at Adam. "I'll take her from here."

Adam looked between us, expression implacable, then nodded and walked away. A few moments later, I realized that the Western Alpha and I were standing completely still, grinning at each other, while an audience of thirty looked on.

"Waiting on you, buddy," I said through my teeth.

Declan glanced around, smile fading a little. "Typical," he muttered, then waved me forward.

———

SEPTEMBER in the Pacific Northwest had a different definition than it did in Southern California. It was freaking cold. I jumped in place to warm my muscles as I waited for Declan to return in running clothes. He'd left me at a trailhead and sprinted back to the sprawling, modern palace that was the Prime's compound.

When I'd told him he didn't have to run with me, he'd given me a flat look and said, "Tell that to my boss."

I decided not to be offended.

I was in the middle of stretching my quads when a rustling alerted me to company. I looked around, but saw nothing save for pine trees and thick undergrowth. It was very quiet, even the birds having ceased their trills.

"Declan?"

Brush moved to my left and I swiveled on my heels, coming face-to-face with a lovely, petite redhead. She was also completely naked.

"Shit," I blurted, averting my eyes.

"Oh my gosh, I'm so sorry!" More rustling, this time of fabric, and then a throaty giggle. "I didn't mean to startle you. I was in wolf form and didn't want to sneak up on you, but completely forgot about the flashing side effect of the change. You can turn around now."

I did, and thankfully she was clothed, albeit in a random outfit—overly large, men's athletic shorts and a sports jersey. Wild red hair sprang from her head in tight coils. Her bright blue eyes were filled with humor and curiosity.

"You're Fiona, right?" she asked, but didn't wait for an affirmative, grabbing my hand and shaking it vigorously. "Dec told me about you. Well, he told all of us. Said you were a cool girl. I'm Tabitha, but everyone calls me Tabby. Like the cat." She grimaced. "It's kinda an insult, seeing that I'm a wolf. But whatever. It's all about perspective, right? I'm fast and agile, like a cat. So I'm okay with it."

I blinked repeatedly, trying to make sense of her rambling. "Uhh—"

Tabitha—Tabby—turned at some noise I didn't hear. "Declan!" she exclaimed with pleasure.

The man in question stepped forward from between two trees, his expression somewhere between chagrined and amused. He avoided my gaze as Tabby skipped forward and threw her arms around his waist, pressing a kiss to his bearded chin.

Ah.

The sudden, deep pang of loneliness in my gut took me by surprise. As Declan returned her embrace, I turned away, both to grant them privacy and to give myself a chance to get my feelings under control.

I didn't know Declan outside the hour we'd spent together last night, and it wasn't like I'd seriously considered having a fling with the man. But despite knowing that a little flirting did not a declaration of love make, now that I'd met Tabby I felt ashamed of my behavior.

The Prime had warned me, but I hadn't listened. I'd been too wrapped up in the possibility of physically being with someone again.

It would have been a lot easier if she was a bitch like Samantha.

"Ready for that run?" asked Declan.

I plastered a smile on my face and turned. "Absolutely. It was great meeting you, Tabby."

She grinned. "Likewise. And if you need anything at all, let me know."

A lightbulb went off in my head. I needed underwear and some clothing besides leggings. And socks. I was banking on the Prime footing the bill; as I saw it, he owed me.

"If that's a serious offer, I actually do need some things. Girl stuff. Is there a mall nearby, and if so, how can I get there?"

Tabby nodded enthusiastically. "It's about a half hour away. If it's okay with Connor, I'd be happy to take you. How's after lunch sound?"

"Connor says that's fine," Declan offered. I shot him an incredulous look and he tapped his temple. "The boss has links to Adam and me."

I shuddered. "Creepy."

Tabby laughed. "It's pretty weird, right? One

time, Connor started talking to Declan in the middle of—"

"Okay," Declan interjected, laughing forcefully. "Time to get moving. Fiona looks cold." He kissed Tabby's temple. "We'll met you in the cafeteria at noon. Connor wants me to tag along." He winked at me. "Wouldn't want our guest to wander off."

I snorted. Tabby nodded happily. "That sounds great, see you then. Have a good run!" She took off at a jog toward the compound, and we watched her go.

After a few moments of pregnant silence, Declan began, "Fiona, I—"

"Whoa." I held up a stalling hand. "No harm, no foul."

"I still feel like I should apologize."

I forced my own laugh. "Great, so you're emotionally mature, too. Way to rub it in."

He made a low noise, very near a growl. I startled at the sight of his eyes, bleeding to yellow and full of heat. I flushed and looked away, trying recall the last time someone had looked at me with such hunger. I couldn't remember.

"Sorry," he said quickly. "You're just, I don't know, so *different*. You bring out the alpha in me, which is odd since you're not a shifter." He paused, and I glanced up to see him dragging a hand through his hair. "I'm probably an asshole for saying this, but shifter relationships are usually open."

I couldn't quite repress a squint of revulsion; I was also grudgingly impressed by his bluntness. Feeling conflicted, I backpedaled into humor.

"This conversation is getting a little intense for me. I haven't even had breakfast yet."

The tension broke and he grinned. "We're okay then?"

"Of course." I narrowed my eyes. "You know, despite popular opinion, men and women are capable of friendship."

His eyes twinkled. "With benefits?"

I groaned. "About that emotionally mature comment…"

He laughed. "Come on, sparky, let's run."

10

LATE THAT EVENING, as I was unpacking three large shopping bags courtesy of the Prime's black American Express, there was a knock on my bedroom door.

"Come in," I called.

The door clicked open. "Hey, kiddo."

I dropped the current bag and ran, launching into my uncle's arms with zero care for my status as a grown woman or the Prime standing behind him.

Mal caught me with an, "Oomph," and laughed, spinning me around before setting me back on my feet. He ruffled my hair, fingers pausing on the streak of white.

"It suits your coloring," he said gruffly.

I smiled halfheartedly. "Who are you and what did you do with my uncle?"

Troubled hazel eyes found mine. "It's good to see you. Let's go over to the library for a chat."

Nerves danced in my belly. Nodding, I followed him into the hallway. The opposite door stood open, emitting murmurs of conversation and the auras of those within.

As much as it pained me to admit, the Prime was right about one thing. My sensitivity to auras had definitely increased, making it easier to distinguish between individuals.

Whereas before I could see but not feel the auras of mages, now I felt the spine-tingling heat of the two Opals and the less potent sting of Mal's Sapphire rank. Declan's heady shifter pulse was also easily identifiable, but there were several others in the room whose auras I didn't know. Two vampires, who felt like sharp jabs of cold air, and another shifter. An alpha, if I wasn't mistaken.

"You look lovely," murmured the Prime.

I mentally catalogued the price of my outfit, then met the amused green gaze. "You'll change your mind when you see the bill."

He smirked, pausing at the door through which Mal had already disappeared. "After you, Fiona."

I crossed the threshold and received nods of greeting from Adam, Declan, and Alisande. At my entrance the three strangers stood, though their deference probably had more to do with the man at my back.

The Prime spoke over my head, "Fiona, meet Charles, Eve, and Matthew. Charles and Eve are masters in Seattle and Matthew is the alpha werebear of this region."

Matthew wasn't the first shifter I'd met who physically resembled his animal form, but in his case, the similarity was pronounced. He was huge and burly, with long, shaggy dark hair and a grizzled beard shot through with gray. His eyes as they met mine, though, were kind, without the usual aggression common to alphas.

The unsmiling vamps could have been twins, both slender and dark-haired, with luminous olive skin. They eyed me like I was a tasty treat, nostrils flaring and dark eyes gleaming.

When the female, Eve, licked her lips hungrily, I took an involuntary step back, straight into the Prime's chest. His fingers curled over my shoulders, lifting goose bumps under my clothes. Whatever the look on his face was, the vamps immediately sat down, eyes lowering.

Neat trick, I thought pointedly, and he gently squeezed my shoulders before releasing me.

"It's nice to meet you, Fiona," said Matthew, eyes a little wide as they veered between the vamps and me. "Though I'm sorry for the circumstances."

"Thanks," I said weakly.

Mal, occupying a chair beside Alisande, said, "Let's begin, shall we?"

Declan and Adam took the second couch, leaving an empty love seat and one chair. I promptly veered toward the chair, set farthest away from the gathering and nearest a dark fireplace.

The Prime sprawled on the love seat, a small, knowing smile on his face and his eyes on Mal. The smile vanished as my uncle began to speak, and I tore my gaze from the vampire.

"Connor, your contact in the FBI was very helpful. The trace on Frank's rental car pinged earlier today. The car was found near Snoqualmie Falls, about fifty minutes from the airport." His gaze flickered to me and away, but not before I saw the despair in them.

"Mal?" I whispered.

Pinched lips told me he'd heard me, but he kept his gaze on the Prime. "There was sign of a struggle but no body."

"Did you sense alchemy?" asked the Omega.

Mal nodded. "Yes, but I don't know if it was from the same source as the signature in Los Angeles. It's like a universal, bad taste in the mouth," he added for the benefit of the non-mages.

Matthew cleared his throat. "I have a few bears living out there. I'd be happy to give them a call to find out if they heard anything or happened to see Frank."

"Thank you," said the Prime, and the shifter rose and lumbered from the room.

"Do we think the Liberati suspected Frank was closing in on them and took him out?" asked Declan, shooting me an apologetic glance.

The Prime shrugged. "It's hard to say. The morning Frank was due to arrive in Seattle, he called me but didn't leave a message. Perhaps he caught a break in the case. Perhaps not. His file in Los Angeles didn't yield any insights."

I felt a pinch of grief. "He's always been horrible at file notes," I said absently.

"There's something else," said Mal, drawing our attentions back to him. "Frank had a secretary, Rosie Young. She's disappeared as well. I was able to check the manifest for Frank's flight, and there was an R. Young on board that morning."

My jaw dropped. "You think Rosie's involved? Impossible."

Mal met my incredulous gaze. "She's a cipher, isn't she?"

I spluttered. "Yes, but she's the mousiest, shyest woman on the planet. She couldn't hurt a fly, much less overpower Dad."

"You don't know that," said Adam.

"Unless she was an alchemist," noted the Prime.

"It's something, at least," added Declan.

I made a noise of frustration and flopped back in my chair. "No way," I muttered. "It's a coincidence. She probably went to Arizona to visit her sister. She's been talking about it for months."

"Arizona?" asked the Prime in a chilling tone.

I frowned. "Yes. Why?"

He looked away. "No reason."

I sent a thought toward him: an image of me strangling him with my bare hands.

One sculpted brow rose.

Mal sighed. "There isn't much else I can do, Connor. I swept the area and didn't pick up any scents, shifter or otherwise. Besides a small amount of blood, the car was clean of evidence. No surveillance or witnesses. Just the note."

My head snapped up. "What note?"

"*Praesent ut libero,*" said the Prime softly, watching me. "Latin for—"

"I know what it means," I interrupted, closing my stinging eyes. "Live to be free."

"It was for you, wasn't it?" The Prime's voice was so gentle it nearly undid me.

"Yes." Stiffening my spine, I looked at Mal. "Do you have it? Can I see it?"

There was a pregnant pause; my stomach bottomed out. "No, kiddo. It was scratched onto the hood of the car. With a claw, by the look of it."

Dear God.

"So he managed to change," murmured Adam.

"Even if it was just his hands," said Declan, "he ought to have done some damage."

"Indeed," said the Prime. "I'll be leaving shortly to determine if Frank spilled cipher blood."

"What will that accomplish?" I asked.

He nodded toward the vamp twins. "Charles and Eve have a highly specialized familial skill. They can glean certain physical characteristics from blood samples."

Alisande spoke up for the first time, "It's too soon."

I had no idea what she was talking about, until the Prime said, "You'll be coming with me, Fiona."

Alisande sighed. "At least bring Adam."

"Why?" I asked.

Mal began, "Connor—"

The Prime stood, effectively silencing the room. I

didn't feel the surge of his power, but saw its immediate effect. Everyone, even Adam, went pale.

Alisande, though visibly affected, wasn't cowed. "You haven't told her," she accused.

This time, I felt the burst of power as a wind that lifted my hair. Some silent command was issued, because the vamps, Declan, and the mages save for Mal rose and filed from the library. The door slammed behind them without being touched.

I looked at the Prime. His expression was impassive as always, but his eye color wavered between emerald and black.

"As Alisande pointed out, Fiona, our conversation last night was interrupted."

"Why are you so angry?" I asked, stupefied.

"Not angry. Frustrated."

I waved a hand. "Whatever. Why are you acting like a prick?"

"Jesus, Fiona," Mal muttered.

A surge of adrenaline brought me to my feet. "Don't start, Mal. It's partly your fault I'm stuck in this mess, falling for that 'her safety for your help' crap. Did you know our illustrious Prime wants to use me like his personal seeing eye dog?"

The instant twist of guilt on my uncle's face felt like a physical blow.

"You knew about this?" I whispered. "For how long?"

He sighed heavily. "Since your first Census. Frank and I knew it was only a matter of time before we had to let you go. You were always meant for great things, kiddo."

With his words, my foundation of support was sundered.

Alone.

I'm one hundred percent alone.

The Prime's lips thinned.

I got angry.

"Has it occurred to either of you how fucked up this is, to put this kind of pressure on me to do something I can't even *conceive* of being able to do? If I can't track the Liberati and Dad ends up dead, where do you think the guilt and responsibility lands? Right here, folks. Thanks to you."

"Has she always been like this?" asked the Prime mutedly.

Mal snorted. "Since she could talk. I blame my brother."

"Fuck you both," I snapped and stormed toward the door. Two feet from it, my nose connected with the Prime's chest. "Out of my way, your highness."

"We'll find him, Fiona."

More words that were weapons. These, arrows

straight to my heart. I clenched my hands, refusing to look up at him.

"You don't know that."

Cool fingers moved through the hair at the base of my neck. His thumbs grazed my jaw, gently tilting my face upward. My mutinous body melted, obeying a biological command for submission.

"Yes, I do. He's alive, and we'll find him."

I stared into his eyes, twin pools of certainty, and opened my mouth to say something caustic. What came out instead was, "Why do you keep touching me?"

Mal cleared his throat and I jerked backward, out of the Prime's reach. Away from his drugging touch. I put a hand to my forehead, feeling flushed and overwhelmed. The men, by some unspoken agreement, waited silently until I pulled myself together.

"Alisande saw something inside me, something that makes her think I can do this?" I asked at length. The Prime nodded. "What did she mean by 'it's too soon'?"

He paused, then admitted, "There's a possibility your ability to track is linked to your lightning. She sensed the potential, but not the manifested power."

"God, I'm a science experiment to you people."

"What you're saying," Mal interjected, "is that

without her lightning, the skill you want to use her for is stunted?"

"Yes."

I took a deep breath and released it. "Then we'd better bring Adam with us."

11

IT WAS a long drive from the compound to Snoqualmie Falls. For the first forty minutes or so, I stared out the back passenger window at the passing greenery, glistening and ripe with shadows in the evening light. Having been born and raised in L.A., the lushness of the landscape was a novelty.

The novelty wore off when the Prime and Omega started arguing.

"I have complete faith in you, Adam."

"I appreciate that," said the Omega flatly, "but it doesn't change the nature of your request. Not even I can stop a bolt of lightning."

"She isn't going to throw one at me." Green eyes, dancing with humor, met mine in the rearview mirror. "Will you, *mo spréach?*"

"Keep up with the pet names and we'll see."

Connor laughed. "See? She wouldn't hurt me. She enjoys our banter far too much."

"I wouldn't be so sure," grumbled Adam. "Besides, it's not that I distrust Fiona, it's that I distrust her discipline."

Despite the growth in our personal relationship from animosity to *not distrust*, I took exception to his statement.

"I went years before Mal perfected the spell to camouflage my charge. I managed fine all by my lonesome."

Which was more or less a lie, unless I measured success as not killing anyone while living in a basement with rubber gym mats attached to the floor and walls. I'd learned to ground, and had slowly built a tolerance for situations and emotions that triggered my charge, but really I just survived.

Nowadays I did my best not to think about that dark time. Ever.

The Prime, of course, knew my thoughts, but Adam didn't. He said contritely, "Those years must have been difficult. May I ask how, exactly, Malcolm's spell aided you?"

I resisted the impulse to refuse. "The spell dampened my charge enough for me to have some semblance of a normal life. Over the years, as my power increased, so did my *discipline*." Adam snorted and I smiled smugly. "The spell grew and changed with me, and became more about averting accidental touch from bystanders. Like a Keep Out sign."

I heard the connotation in the words as soon as I spoke them, and was grateful for the dim car interior. Not that I could hide the rise of my body temperature from the Prime.

The men were silent for all of ten seconds, then burst out laughing.

"Grow up!" I snapped. It was only a few moments, though, before I felt my lips quirk. "Assholes."

"She's laughing," murmured Adam.

Passing headlights illumined the Prime's crinkled eyes in the mirror. "Yes, she is. Like I said, marvelously resilient."

"She'd have to be to survive the initial lightning strike."

I rolled my eyes. "If you're going to talk about me like I'm not here, can we at least turn on some music?"

A button was pressed on the console and Chopin's nocturnes for piano floated from speakers behind my head. I sighed in pleasure and caught a pleased smile in the rearview.

After a few minutes of mellow silence, Adam asked, "Have you considered having Declan teach her the fundamentals of physical tracking? Perhaps it would create a framework of reference for when she comes into her power."

"I have considered it, yes."

"And?"

There was a long pause. "I'd like to see if she can mature intuitively first, without muddying the waters."

Adam's grunt sounded suspiciously like laughter.

"Fiona," said the Prime, "I know you're listening. Distract me from the monotony of the road."

Adam barked a short laugh. "That means he doesn't want to talk to me anymore."

"Fiona? How was lunch?"

My bubble of Chopin-inspired peace burst. "It was fantastic," I said with feigned levity. "Everyone was so welcoming and kind. I especially enjoyed your girlfriend accidentally spilling her scalding blood-coffee on me."

Silence.

I settled back to listen to the music.

"We're here," said Adam, voice reedy with relief.

We'd left the highway ten minutes ago and now rolled to a stop on a dark, narrow road. Trees clogged the skyline around us, blotting out the stars and the sliver of moon.

The Prime didn't wear a seat belt and was out of

the car first. Before following, Adam turned from the passenger seat to face me.

"If you lose control, I'm going to surround you in a ward that will contain your power. I'm telling you now because you won't be able to escape. Don't try. Do you understand?"

I nodded. Making sure my voice was firm, I told him, "I won't hurt the Prime." As an afterthought, I added, "Or you."

He watched me for a moment, then nodded shortly. We exited the car and walked toward the Prime, who was pacing the road with measured steps.

"He's searching for the scent of blood."

"I got that from the sniffing noises."

Adam grunted, mouth twitching. For several more minutes the Prime continued pacing, then he stiffened and turned, striding swiftly from the road onto damp dirt and pine needles.

Squatting, he lowered his face until it hovered an inch from the ground. "Here," he snapped. "Get the kit. It's an infinitesimal sample, but I think I can capture it."

Adam raced to the trunk, returning moments later with a small duffel bag. I hung back, leaning against the warm hood of the car. The cold was deep and piercing, its fingers climbing beneath my wool coat. I had a sudden, powerful longing for the mild nights of home.

I tried very hard not to think about the blood on the ground.

The Prime collected his sample, Adam stored it, and the bag was returned to the trunk. I hugged my arms to my chest and watched the vampire, who was staring into the dark woods. His face was shadowed, but I could see coiled tension in his shoulders.

"What is it?" asked Adam.

"Something…" He shook his head. "Nothing. My imagination. Come here, Fiona."

"Yes, master," I muttered and pushed off the car.

On my second step, a queer tingling took ahold of my limbs. "What the—"

"Alchemy!" yelled Adam. "Connor!"

The space where the Prime had been standing emptied a millisecond before an explosion tore upward. Fire, earth, and metal debris shot into the air, peppering the nearest trees and tearing chunks of bark from their trunks.

I was on my knees, coughing in a cloud of dirt, without memory of falling. My ears were ringing and I tasted blood in my mouth.

That odd, tingling sensation returned with a vengeance. Like nails on a chalkboard times ten.

"Adam," I gasped. "It's happening ag—"

Arms grabbed me. My head spun and my vision blurred. A heady *boom* sounded somewhere close by and a blistering wave of heat cascaded over my back. I whimpered, and the heat stopped. Blocked, I realized, by the man holding me.

"I've got you. Just breathe."

"The car," gasped Adam.

"Fuck the car," snapped the Prime. "I can't hear any heartbeats besides yours and Fiona's. Are they here, or did they set the trap and leave?"

A low groan of pain and aggravation came from Adam. "I don't know," he whispered. "Something hit me in the head. Run, Connor. Take Fiona."

"I'm not leaving you."

He set me on my feet, grabbing my shoulder when I wavered. Something wet trickled down my temple and I touched it, my fingers coming away dark with blood.

"Protect her. If they're here, I'll find them."

"No, Connor—"

He was gone.

"Dammit," Adam hissed, his head falling back against a tree trunk.

Some twenty feet away, the glow of the burning car was visible through trees. A bead of sweat ran down my back. My arms itched horribly. And that damned tingling was back, rising to a high-pitched whine in my ears.

"Adam—"

His eyes went white. "I sense it." He grabbed my arm, forcing me behind him. "Stay down. If I'm taken out, you have to run. Fast, Fiona."

"Take off the bracelets," I panted. "Let me help."

Light flashed through the trees and a cry of pain echoed in the night.

Adam made a strangled noise and ran toward the sound. White radiance glowed around him, building in intensity until I had to squint to see the shape of him inside it. Belatedly, I realized the cry had come from the Prime.

The itching in my arms reached new heights, morphing into a steady burn. I tore off my jacket to stare at the silver ribbons dancing on my skin. I didn't feel the electricity—not yet—but *holy shit* it hurt.

The bracelets began to brighten, the metal heating. The scent of my burning flesh hit me an instant before the pain. I dropped to my knees with a muffled scream.

Pressure built in my spine until my back bowed. The power inside me writhed and bucked against its constraints.

My father's voice whispered in my mind.

Praesent ut libero…

Live to be free.

The bracelets withered and turned to ash.

CRACK.

I went blind at the first expulsion of energy, barely managing to keep my palms angled toward the ground. The base of the nearest tree split in half, sparks and gouts of smoke billowing from its remains. Gasping, I clenched my hands and ground my teeth.

Stay with me, I told the lightning. *Not yet.*

I didn't think. I scrambled to my feet and ran, following the shimmering trail of the Omega's magic. When I reached the tree line, I crouched behind a trunk and peered out at the road.

I saw the Prime first, lying on his side in a pool of blood, fifteen feet from the smoking car. He was angled away from me. By his stillness, he was either unconscious or dead.

Adam was a pillar of white radiance between the Prime and a line of three men in black camo. Disjointed blue sparkles filled the air around the Liberati, darting like erratic stars. The central figure held an unnaturally smooth sphere, about the size of a basketball. In the glowing, milky depths was a wriggling crimson snake with fluorescent green eyes and a forked tongue.

What. The. Unholy. Fuck.

A flash of white and a *snap* was followed by one of the Liberati falling to his knees. He shook himself and rose back to his feet, even the magic of an Opal Mage repelled by his cipher defenses. Adam had no such protection. The crystal sphere flared bright red, the snake lashing from side to side. Adam cried out, his corona flickering wildly before bouncing back to full strength.

"Give us the girl, Omega, and we'll let you live!"

Wait—*what?*

I looked down at my arms, lit up like the Fourth of July, and knew once I appeared I'd be immediately visible. That freaky alchemy would head my way, without any assurances that the Omega would protect me.

In fact, I wouldn't blame him if he grabbed the Prime and ran. He didn't know me or owe me loyalty. Regardless of the Prime's convictions, right now I was a liability that could get them both killed.

It wasn't a choice, really.

I stepped out from behind the tree. Immediately, four sets of eyes snapped my way. I guess I was brighter than I'd thought.

"Dammit, Fiona," snarled Adam, apparently more irritated that I'd disobeyed him than that I'd obliterated his spell.

"Fiona Sullivan," spoke the central man, his bald head gleaming in the firelight. "Come with us. We are not your enemy. Your father is safe and waiting for you."

The lies stung like wasps. My arms burned. My palms burned. My whole body, toes to crown, burned with white-hot rage.

The first lightning bolt missed, striking a tree with a rending screech of wood. The second was deflected at the last second by the crystal sphere. The third, however, found its mark, ricocheting off the ground and slamming into the leftmost man. He didn't make a sound as his body flew backward and crumpled against a tree.

"You'll regret this!" screamed the bald man. "Before your father dies, I'll tell him you could have saved him!"

Pain seared my heart. My arms pulsed and I lifted them.

"You don't know my father very well."

I released the lightning and it hit empty asphalt where the man had been standing. The bolt veered skyward, piercing the darkness and for a moment, illuminating the road.

The Liberati were gone.

I sagged, arms falling limp and dark to my sides.

The smell of ozone was thick. Fire flickered in the forest as the tree I'd first struck went up in flames.

I looked helplessly at Adam and he lifted his arms, his eyes flashing white. Moisture filled the air, thick and foggy on my face. A moment later, warm rain began to fall, sizzling against the charred car and smothering the fires. Along with the smells of damp earth, charred wood, and burning metal, there was a strange buzzing in the air.

"Do you feel that?" I asked Adam. "A weird vibration?"

He gave me a penetrating look. "No, but I'm pretty sure you're sensing the magical resonance of alchemy."

The statement brought me back to the present, and to the Prime. I stumbled to him and dropped to my knees. Blood masked his throat and chest, though whatever wound had caused it was already healed.

He was pale. Too pale. Dark bruises marred the skin beneath his closed eyes.

Footsteps approached, squelching wetly on the road. "He needs blood," said Adam wearily.

"Okay," I whispered, rain misting from my lips. "Yours or mine?"

"Yours. The blood of mages is unpalatable to vampires."

"Huh. Lucky you."

"Here," he said and handed me a small, wicked looking knife.

Feeling strangely calm—shock was a beautiful thing—I sliced the skin of my wrist above the circular burn from Adam's bracelet. Blood welled and was washed away by the rain.

I pushed my wrist to the Prime's mouth. His body jerked, curling around my arm. A small sigh escaped him. Dark eyelashes flickered, then parted on black eyes. His fangs struck.

It didn't hurt like I thought it would. There was no venom, not like a snakebite or the sting of a bee. Just a pinch, then numbness.

Then sucking.

After the third or fourth pull, he regained some measure of consciousness. Enough to make noises that brought heat to my face and pooled low in my body.

I closed my eyes and tried to think of pleasant, platonic things. Running on the beach at dawn. A hot cup of tea and a good book. Pizza. Chihuahuas.

"That's enough," said Adam sharply, but Connor's grip only tightened, a low growl in his throat.

My aches and pains floated away on a red haze. Everything was wonderful. Perfect. There was nowhere else I wanted to be. I giggled and listed to one side, and finally fell. I felt no impact. The wet asphalt was soft and sparkly, a bed of glittering pillows.

My eyelids parted just enough for me to see Connor Thorne's beautiful, enraptured face, and my wrist tucked firmly in his mouth.

Adam yelled, "Stop now or you'll kill her!"

His eyes snapped open, pupils blown wide and filled with a night sky. Millions of stars, flickering and streaking through unrelieved black.

"Pretty," I whispered.

Reality shifted, bent, and swirled down the drain.

12

I OPENED my eyes on a windswept, rocky shoreline. There was a small islet of golden sand beneath my feet, a safe haven between the forbidding, storm-swept sea and jagged black rocks. In the distance, green hills gave way to towering, majestic mountains.

"I'm sorry, Fiona."

His voice didn't surprise me. Nothing about this surprised me.

I turned to face the Prime. He was soaking wet, his hair a tangled mess and blood still streaking his neck. His black blouse and slacks were plastered to him, highlighting contours of muscle and not leaving much to the imagination.

I looked quickly at his face. "Am I dying?"

"No, just recovering." His eyes lost their

solemnness, flaring with laughter. "I wasn't apologizing for biting you, by the way."

"Taste as good as I smell, do I?"

A corner of his mouth curled, pressing a dimple into one cheek. "Better, actually."

I sighed. "Fantastic."

He took a step toward me. "Your hair..." He stilled, frowning. "How many bolts did you throw?"

I swallowed. "It's all white, isn't it?"

"Yes."

I reached back, pulling my long ponytail into view. Bleached strands stuck together wetly. Sighing, I threw the hair over my shoulder.

"It's like a nonstop roller coaster of fun with you."

He made a low noise of mingled humor and pain. "I'm sorry I didn't protect you."

"Oh, stop it," I snapped. "Clearly I can protect myself."

He smiled cheekily. "Clearly."

I turned my head to gaze into the distance. The silence became weighted. I didn't feel like talking about what had happened. Didn't want to confront the Liberati's threat regarding my father. Or admit that despite my near-certainty that he'd been lying, I'd chosen the Prime and Omega over my dad.

"He was lying, Fiona. There was no other choice to make."

"Like I just *thought*, I don't want to talk about it."

"Did you sense the alchemy this time?"

I started nodding, then froze and scowled at him. "I still don't want to talk. At least let me process everything first."

"I'm sorry."

Heat snaked down my arms, pooling in my hands. I clenched my fingers. "Couldn't you let me sleep? Did you have to drag me into your little dreamworld?"

Those damnable lips twitched. "Sorry?"

I shouted in wordless frustration and kicked the ground, sending a spray of sand against his legs. He merely laughed.

Giving in to the ultimate temptation, I loosed a small streak of lightning, zapping him in the stomach. He shuddered and bent in half. Guilt bloomed and worry had me running the space between us.

"Connor, are you okay? I'm so sorry!"

Then I heard the sound he was making. He'd bent in half *laughing*.

"Gah!" I shoved his shoulder as hard as I could, catching him off balance and sending him flying back onto the sand. Moving too fast for my eye to follow, he snagged my leg and I teetered, then collapsed on top of him with a screech.

I glared down at his grinning face. "Why is everything so goddamn funny to you?"

His mirth softened and he blinked. "There's only so much grief a person can withstand. I reached my limit a long time ago. It was either choose humor, or choose the sun."

A chill touched my neck. "You would have killed yourself?"

He nodded. Though his eyes stayed pale green, they reflected dark memories. "Yes. And now, with Ascension, that option has been taken from me. If you live to be as old as I am, perhaps you'll understand."

"You almost died tonight," I objected.

"No, I didn't. Every last drop of blood could be drained from me and I would still live, a comatose and withered husk. Unless someone took my head, that is."

I glanced down at his chest. "What about a stake through the heart?"

"That only kills young ones."

I looked back into his eyes, then trailed my gaze down his imperfect nose, over his mouth and the shadow of facial hair on his jaw. They were all merely pieces of the whole, minutiae of one of the most complex, formidable men on the planet. A being old enough to have experienced a measure of sorrow miles beyond the norm.

I imagined losing Michael, over and over again, and touched upon a small fraction of what the Prime was talking about. If I'd had to watch my loved ones grow old and die ad nauseam, I could easily envision locking my heart behind walls of indifference.

Hell, it'd been locked for fourteen years. What was another thousand?

"Do you even care?" I asked, my voice raw. "About finding my dad? About anything?"

"Yes," he murmured. "I care."

The curtain of impassivity dropped from his eyes and my brain finally caught up with the implication of our positions. My breasts were pressed against his chest, his hands lightly gripping my hips. My heart pulsed hard—once, twice—and flooded me with sensation.

Heat. *Want*.

Electricity erupted from my skin. Connor groaned, but not in pain.

"I'm sorry," I gasped and shoved off his chest, scrambling backward so fast I tripped and fell on my ass. My breath expelled in a rush, pain zigging up my spine.

I sensed movement and looked up at Connor—

no, the *Prime*—standing with his hands in the pockets of his slacks, an indecipherable expression on his face.

"Time to wake up, Fiona."

"FIONA, TIME TO WAKE UP."

Fingers stroked my forehead, imparting a pulsing warmth. I cracked open my eyes to see Declan leaning over me. He smiled, pale eyes sparkling.

"Hey," I said weakly.

He disappeared and appeared again with a glass of water. Lifting my shoulders with one arm, he held the rim to my lips. Cool water cleansed my tongue and throat.

I swallowed reflexively until the glass was empty. "Thank you."

"You're welcome," he said, depositing the glass on the side table. "How do you feel?"

I glanced past him, seeing a stormy sky outside the windows of my room in the compound. "Like I was bulldozed then set on fire." I paused. "My hair? Did I dream…?"

"It was no dream," he said gently. "It's white. Kinda sexy, actually. Really shiny and soft."

His teasing brought more memory back, of the

Prime and a beach. *Has it been real?* In turn, I was forced to acknowledge there was only one way Declan could be touching me with impunity.

I lifted my arms and stared at the new, thicker bracelets on my wrists.

"Dammit."

"It was for everyone's protection," said Declan softly. "You were unconscious and throwing sparks whenever anyone came near you. You killed the engines of five cars on the way back to the compound."

I winced. "I'm surprised they even started."

"It took some experimenting, but Connor finally figured out if he held you and absorbed your surges, it spared the engine."

"Absorbed my—God, is he okay?"

He grinned. "Fine. Adam was the most freaked out by it, but he finally decided you can't hurt Connor because he's so damned old and basically dead. His heart beats once every five minutes or something crazy like that. The worst you did was increase his heart rate to once a minute."

I didn't feel an inkling of Declan's humor. "And the bracelets? Didn't I prove myself to Adam last night?"

His smile fell. "Connor was the one who ordered Adam to replace them. He said that you'd want them." He frowned worriedly. "Was that not true?"

I had no idea how to answer his question. Or what I was feeling.

Confused was an understatement.

The Prime and our disturbing moment of intimacy aside, I suddenly missed my old life with a vengeance. I missed my tiny apartment. My boring job and my own shampoo.

And I missed my dad, with a depth that felt like a knife in my heart. I missed his gruff voice and the way he chewed his mustache when he was thinking. I wanted to hear his laughter, gravelly and deep, and listen to him yell at the television during his favorite sports games. I just *missed* him.

Grief was bright and dark, a polarized force that swayed me between hope and despair. Was he dead already? Had it been his blood catalyzing that unnatural crystal sphere?

I knew it was foolish, but I also couldn't help wondering if I should have gone with those men. If I could have freed my dad and brought him home.

I almost asked Declan where Uncle Mal was and if I could see him. But the twisting hurt I felt was too raw. He'd known the Prime would come for me. All those years he'd supposedly been protecting me, he'd actually been protecting an asset for someone else. If my safety had been of primary concern, he would've convinced my father to move us to the middle of nowhere. Change our names. Hide.

I refused to believe my dad had known.

Absolutely refused.

There was a knock on the door and Declan rose, but instead of veering to the entrance he walked to a second door, set between the fireplace and the bank of windows. A door I'd avoided thinking about until this moment. It opened as he turned a thick, pewter key already resting in the lock beneath an embellished handle.

Soft words were exchanged between Alpha and Prime.

"She's fine," murmured Declan. "Beat up emotionally." A pause. "We've really done a number on her."

"I know. Nothing has gone as expected."

"Can you give it a few days before taking her back to Snoqualmie?"

"We're not going back. Adam checked the area twice. Whatever alchemy the Liberati performed when they vanished, it wiped their tracks as well."

"Damn, they're like ghosts. Anything from Matthew, or word on Frank's secretary?"

"The bears saw and heard nothing, and local police in Phoenix are checking out the sister."

Declan sighed. "What now?"

"Charles and Eve have the blood sample we salvaged from the car. It will take a few days for results, but given the trap the Liberati set, the blood could have come from anyone. For now we wait, and in the meantime, Fiona will train."

I lifted onto my elbows and looked across the room. "Train?"

The Prime's gaze scanned my face before settling on my eyes. His own were devoid of their usual wryness. Everything about him seemed blank.

"You've demonstrated an instinctive talent for releasing lightning, but Adam mentioned you missed your targets twice. We've secured a location where you can explore your range and hone your skills."

Missed your targets.

The words rang dully in my ears, triggering recollection of one target I hadn't missed.

I blinked hard when the Prime's face blurred. "I killed a man, didn't I?"

He nodded. "In self-defense, yes."

"Was it?" I asked softly, searching his eyes for any hint of feeling. Compassion or humor, irony or sorrow. Anything at all to confirm that the man on the beach was real. That it hadn't been a dream. I had no idea what I would do with the information, but I wanted to know.

His eyes remained void of emotion—flat, spring green. Which, consequently, was all the answer I needed. It had been real. And he regretted it. He'd likely been drunk on my blood, which apparently ramped up a vamp's... other needs. Nothing more.

Nothing more.

"It was self-defense," he said finally. Breaking eye contact, he looked at Declan. "Bring her to the east wing in two hours."

He vanished and Declan closed the door.

"Lock it," I said.

He did.

13

MY APPEARANCE in the main hall of the compound yielded different results this time around. People still stared, still whispered. But they also nodded. Some of the mages even bowed.

"What's the party line?" I hissed at Declan as we veered down a hallway.

He glanced at me, brows lifted. "You saved the lives of the Prime and Omega. That's a pretty big deal."

I gaped. "Adam was holding his own. They would have been fine."

"I call Denial," he quipped. "Even if Adam had run the Liberati off and found someone to feed Connor, what you did was impressive as hell. *Lightning,* Fiona. There's no record of anyone like you existing, before or after Ascension. There's talk in the compound and beyond. Word about you is getting out."

"What? What word?" I asked shrilly.

Panic softened the edges of my vision and I paused, leaning on a nearby wall for support. Thankfully, we were alone in a spacious hallway, with no one to witness my meltdown.

"Hey," he said, framing my face with his hands. "It's *good* word." His thumbs grazed my cheekbones. "Even the vamps are impressed, and they're assholes."

It worked. I cracked a smile.

Declan grinned and dropped a quick, hot kiss on my forehead. While I blinked dumbly, he grabbed my hand and tugged me into motion.

"What was that for?" I asked at length.

His bright gaze slanted to me. "Shifters are highly physical. We like to touch a lot. And you, Fiona Sullivan, are starved for touch."

"I don't know whether to be offended or flattered."

He grinned. "Just accept it for the truth. I like touching you, and as long as those bracelets are on, I'm going to keep touching you. Don't worry, I have the utmost respect for your boundaries."

Mind reeling, I barely noticed as we drew to a halt beside a thick, iron bracketed door. Finally, I looked down at our entwined hands. Seeing. Feeling. His palm was lightly calloused, warm and encompassing. I squeezed his fingers and he squeezed back, imparting a pervasive warmth.

Declan was right. I was starved for touch. Simple, uncomplicated affection from someone other than my uncle. My dad had never been the warm and fuzzy type, but even he had been restricted from touching me since Ascension.

"Thank you," I whispered.

"Come here," he murmured and drew me forward.

His arms enfolded me, tight and solid, one palm cupping the back of my head. The steady beat of his heart sounded beneath my ear. Tension melted from my body and I drew a deep breath, pulling his scent into my greedy lungs. He smelled like the wild, like fresh air and shadowed woods.

There was no expectation in the touch, just affection freely given. It was a revelation.

"Well, isn't this cozy," said a saccharine voice.

Declan gave me a final squeeze before releasing me, and we both looked at Samantha, watching us from the open doorway. Behind her, some fifteen feet away in a massive, white-walled room, standing on what looked like a gymnastics mat, was the Prime.

My face burned with embarrassment. It was completely misplaced—I had nothing to be ashamed of—but I couldn't repress it any more than I could manifest a stake punching through Samantha's heart. Or every frosted blond hair falling from her head. Or a lit pyre beneath her stilettoed feet.

"It's really too bad you can't dye that," she said, smirking at my hair.

The Prime growled, "Samantha."

She bowed her head and moved past us, but quipped over her shoulder, "You could always try a wig."

I watched her sashay away, the sway of her hips so contrived that amusement washed away my anger.

"She's a real piece of work," muttered Declan.

Connor sighed. "Fiona, come inside, please."

I smiled weakly at Declan; he tugged my ponytail. "See you later. Have fun."

As soon as I entered the training room, the door clicked closed. I gazed around the expansive, windowless space, completely empty but for the mat in the center of the floor. Sparkling along the walls and ceiling was dense white magic.

"Adam assured me the ward would keep your lightning inside," said the Prime.

"I don't doubt it," I replied, finally looking at him. "Why is your girlfriend such a bitch?"

His eyelids flickered. "She feels threatened by you."

I blinked, taken aback by his candor. "Because I'm staying in the Consort's suite?" He nodded. "I'm surprised you're not dating someone with a little more backbone."

Amusement flared in his eyes. "Has it occurred to you I might not appreciate being challenged by a lover?"

"No, actually," I said, then snapped my mouth shut.

His expression went blank. "Let's begin. Remove the bracelets."

I looked at my wrists and back at him. "What? How?"

"There are release catches located on each."

I launched into action, finding and pressing small, etched runes at the base of each bracelet. They parted with a soft *pop* and fell to the ground. Electricity surged through me, bending my spine and tearing a moan from my throat.

I was whole.

There'd be time later to examine the double-edged blade currently swinging. One side: Declan's warm touch and a part of me missing. And the other: feeling complete, but cut off from physical affection.

Well, from everyone save the Western Prime.

While I stood basking in my current, the Prime crossed the space between us and took position behind me.

"Hit the targets, please."

I descended from my musings to see his index finger outstretched toward the opposite wall. Three large bull's-eyes were painted on the white surface, spaced several feet apart, with four rings around each central point.

I ignored them for the moment, turning to stare at him. He sighed, lowering his arm. "Yes?"

"Did absorbing my charges really not hurt you, or were you pretending for Adam's sake?"

He fixed me with a dispassionate gaze. "I'd rather not discuss it."

"So they did hurt you."

"No."

"No, what? No, they didn't hurt you, or no, you aren't talking about it?"

His eyes flashed to emerald. Call me sick and twisted, but I was glad to have provoked him.

"You're trying my patience."

I shrugged. "What else is new?"

A muscle ticked in his jaw, which made me smile. Yep, there was something seriously wrong with me.

"You know very well it doesn't hurt me," he growled. "Moreover, if the ride back to the compound was any indication, your blood enhanced my immunity."

"I've never actually hit you with lightning. Not in real life, at least."

He took a menacing step toward me. I took a quick step back. Fangs flashed behind his lips. "I wouldn't finish that line of thought if I were you."

Adrenaline zinged through me, blotting out my worry, my fear—all the dark, helpless feelings I kept buried moment to moment.

The Prime's eyes narrowed. "There are better ways to cope with your emotions."

The words hit home, instantly deflating my mood. "You're right. I'm sorry." I turned away to stare at one of the bull's-eyes.

He said softly, "I have to attend an event tonight in Seattle. I'd like you to come as a part of my security retinue. It will be an excellent opportunity for you to practice tracking."

"That's like telling me to practice my Swahili," I muttered.

"You've tracked mages before, with your father."

I sighed, shaking my head. "With credit card receipts and investigative work." I faced him, scowling. "What if I'm not, in fact, capable of tracking magical resonance?"

"You are," he said sharply. He pointed behind me. "Hit the targets."

Anger brought heat and electricity surging down my arms and into my hands. I turned on my heel and released a bolt.

It hit the ceiling.

"Again."

The next one careened off the rubber mat, sizzling out with a muted flash.

"Again."

"Shut up," I snarled and funneled more power. I missed spectacularly, three times in a row. "Fuck!"

Fingers curled over my shoulders and a hard chest met my back. His breath tickled my ear as he said, "In the heat of battle, emotions surge. Fear, rage, horror. Discipline allows us to use these emotions to elevate our skills."

"Stop touching me," I snapped.

He did the opposite, moving his hands around my neck and clasping the column lightly. Lips grazed my ear and goose bumps bloomed over my chest.

"Do not mistake me for Declan," he whispered, and I felt the kiss of fangs along my earlobe. I shuddered. "Nothing about me is warm. Little enough is human. I am going to use you to get what I want. And if you keep testing the boundaries between us, I'm going to use you in other ways. Ways that, from your scent even now, you will greatly enjoy. Do you understand?"

Animal arousal plummeted through me. Every nerve in my body went hyperaware, my senses unfurling, purring at his strength, his scent, his nearness.

Then my brain entered the battle ring and took out desire with a blinding right hook.

I was a fool.

A fool who'd fallen prey to the manufactured charm and predatory glamour of an ancient vampire. A fool who looked for him in every room I entered, who constantly sought his notice, and ways to make him smile and laugh.

Holy shit.

I had Stockholm syndrome.

"I understand that you're a manipulative bastard," I told him. My voice only shook a little. "I understand nothing about you is authentic. That you're a machine with a dead heart."

His fingers left my throat. "Machines don't have hearts," he said flatly. "Now use your anger to focus. Hit the targets."

I didn't hit them—I obliterated them, the wall they were painted on, and Adam's ward. And as plaster dust rained down, and the mild autumn sunlight glinted through the hole blown in the side of the compound, the Prime laughed, his eyes twinkling and bright.

Grinning down at me, he said, "You are everything I hoped for and more, *mo spréach*."

Panting and shaking from fatigue, I weighed the chances I might pass out if I tried for another bolt, this time aimed at him. "What does that mean?"

He didn't pretend to misunderstand. "*Mo spréach* is Gaelic for 'my spark.' Because you are both."

A spark. And *his*.

I was mildly surprised to find that, indeed, I still had energy for anger.

"You and Samantha deserve each other."

Nothing. Not even a flicker of eyelashes.

"I've never lied to you. Not once. Hate me if you will, but I'm the only chance you have to see your father again."

"Fuck you."

Between one blink and the next, his fingers gripped my jaw. My face was yanked upward, giving me no choice but to stare into glittering black eyes. For the very first time in his presence, I felt real fear.

His nostrils flared and his voice came as a hiss

through fangs. "I see through you, Fiona Sullivan. I see every layer of your mind and heart. And yet, somehow, you confound me at every turn. Aggravate me. Challenge me. For all your resiliency, you lack basic instinct when it comes to me. Perhaps it is because I have withheld my aura from you. Or perhaps I have been too familiar. Too kind. There are compelling reasons why I'm respected and obeyed. Once, long ago, I was worshipped. You would do well to remember that."

Against all my efforts, tears filled my eyes. "You're scaring me," I whispered. "Why are you doing this?"

The black in his eyes was swallowed by green. His expression was suddenly tortured, so much that I cried out softly. He swallowed hard, the grip on my face slackening.

"To protect you," he said roughly.

I blinked and he was gone, and I stared at the space he'd occupied until I heard a soft throat-clearing. I looked numbly across the room at Adam, standing just inside the door.

"Will you come with me, Fiona? We need to talk."

Something in his tone overcame my need to crawl in a hole and cry.

"Can we go outside?" I asked weakly. "I need some air."

"Of course."

I retrieved my bracelets and snapped them on, only wincing a little as my charge disappeared. Other parts of me hurt worse.

14

ADAM LED me farther down the hallway, around a few turns, and out a side entrance. Our shoes crunched over dead leaves and damp gravel as we crossed a small courtyard. In the center stood a weathered fountain, its tiers empty of water. A frigid wind blew past, lifting leaves into a frenzy and not so much drying my sweat as freezing it.

"Are you cold?" asked Adam. "We can go inside."

"No," I said quickly. "I'm fine. What did you want to talk about?"

He motioned to an iron bench backed by a vine-covered brick wall. I sat beside him, wincing at the cold metal, and a moment later magic flared. Winter was replaced by a tropical jungle; around our bench, at least.

"That's so nice." I slouched against the now-warm seat. "Thanks."

Adam nodded, his dark gaze fixed on the fountain. "I need to tell you some things about Connor."

Physical and emotional exhaustion were apparently a winning combination, because I abruptly saw the situation through unveiled eyes. My dad called such moments the right-sizing of the ego. In other words, the usually accidental process of being humbled.

"Don't bother," I said with a wan smile. "You don't have to justify his behavior. He was right to remind me who he is. The Western-freaking-Prime. I haven't treated him with the respect due his age and power, and he's given me a lot of leeway thus far. I finally crossed the line enough times that he redrew it." I shook my head. "I just want my dad back, Adam. He's been missing for seven days. What have we accomplished toward that goal? Nothing."

"Of course you're worried and unsettled by being here," he said softly. I glanced sharply at him; this was a new Omega, almost *nice*-sounding. "As of this morning, we've handed your father's case to the FBI, with assurances that it will be given priority attention."

"That's actually very reassuring," I said softly. "Thank you for telling me."

"You're welcome." He sighed. "I know you don't want to talk about Connor, but I think we need to." I started shaking my head, but he continued, "It starts with your mother, Delilah."

For close to a minute, I sat completely still, my mind strangely fuzzy. Finally, I nodded.

"Twenty-five years ago, Delilah was in Seattle. Connor had no idea who she was, but for days she kept appearing in the same locations as he—the theater, a park, the bar at the top of the Space Needle. Needless to say, Connor wasn't the Prime then. Nor was he a daywalker. He confronted your mother when she tried following him home one night. He threatened her. He, uh, bit her."

"So much for his fast."

"He didn't drink from her. But he did taste her blood." He paused. "I realize that's a fine line."

I didn't say anything. I was having a Zen moment. The bottom of the world was about to drop out and I was going to serenely watch happen.

Adam cleared his throat and shifted on the bench, as though summoning courage for his next words. "Her blood didn't taste human. She wasn't a mage or shifter, though. She was something other. Your mother… she has a gift."

The surface of my calm shivered, cracks appearing. "What kind of gift?" I asked.

"She can see the future."

Not what I'd been expecting.

"She's psychic? As in palm reading and tarot cards?"

He shook his head. "No, I mean actual precognition. That was how she found Connor. She could glimpse where he would be at any future time. This all happened pre-Ascension, too. Now, her skills are greatly honed. She can find anyone, at any time, anywhere."

I jolted to my feet. "Get her on the goddamn phone! She can find my father!"

He looked at me with such sympathy that I immediately wanted to punch something. "No one has seen or heard from her in years. Connor has been looking for her without success since the first whispers of the Liberati."

Like tendons had been cut, I collapsed back to the bench. "If she's some super psychic, like you say, then she probably knows my dad is missing, maybe hurt or worse, and is doing fuck-all about it."

"Unless something has happened to her, then yes, that's a possibility."

I dropped my chin to my chest, then straightened

as something horrible occurred to me. I stared at Adam unblinking until my eyes burned.

"Does Connor think I have Delilah's skill?" He said nothing, which was answer enough. I laughed hoarsely. "Are you kidding me? All this focus on me tracking resonance is just a smokescreen while he waits for me to manifest some crazy psychic power? Has everyone been lying to me?"

"Fiona—" he began resignedly.

My breath whistled through clenched teeth. "Wow. I thought Delilah Greer had done damage when she abandoned her family, but that was nothing. A cake walk. This whole situation is her doing."

Adam said softly, "Connor believes you can track magical resonance because the night before Delilah left, she told him you could. She also told him you have her Sight. I was there, Fiona. I heard what she said. I have no reason to think she was lying."

"Because you're a sucker," I snapped.

"No. Because much of what has happened since Los Angeles, she predicted that night."

The tension in my neck crackled as I turned my head toward him. "Explain."

"Your hair turning white, the death of the Liberati agent, you freely offering blood to Connor... more random details, all of which have come to pass.

But the larger message was this: she told Connor you would either be the catalyst of his success, or that of his failure. That without you, everything we've worked so hard to build would crumble."

"Wow. No pressure," I muttered.

"Fiona." He said my name in a strange tone, both pleading and foreboding. It got my attention, dragging me out of a vortex of resentment. "There was someone else there that night, who heard Delilah's words. Her name was Gabriella. Connor was her sire—he made her a vampire some fifty years before Ascension. It's her room you're occupying now."

I scanned his face. "Past tense?" I asked softly.

"She was taken by the Liberati eight years ago."

"Oh... Oh."

"Gabriella was kind and gentle. The most passive vampire I've ever met. If it hadn't been for Connor's blood..." He shrugged. "As you know, no vampire under three hundred lived through Ascension, and even then, a third of the Ancients didn't survive. Gabriella would have assuredly died, but instead, she joined Connor as a daywalker."

I looked at the sky, where heavy-bellied clouds moved swiftly southward. I wasn't sure I wanted to know, but asked anyway, "What happened to her?"

"She volunteered several times a week at a

botanical garden in the city. One day, she went to the gardens and never came back."

"How do you know it was the Liberati?"

He paused. "We don't, not with certainty. But they prey on the weakest among us, and Gabriella was that. She would not have willingly left Connor, ever."

My heart hurt.

My brain hurt.

"Why are you telling me this?" I asked.

He dragged a hand down his face, scratching the blond stubble on his jaw. "Connor is a complex man. Even I, his right hand for nearly thirteen years, sometimes think I don't know him at all. If he grieved when Gabriella disappeared, no one saw it. What I did notice, however, was a growing fixation."

I got a funny feeling in my stomach.

Adam nodded at the frozen expression on my face. "Yes, with you. Even before Delilah spoke of you, he knew who you were. There was a bidding war of sorts between Primes when you participated in the first Census. Connor happened to be in Los Angeles that day. He won the rights to you by proximity and wouldn't back down when the others wanted to meet you. They would have offered you anything you wanted, taken you from your home, and turned you into a weapon."

Isn't that what Connor's doing?

But I didn't ask. I sat very still. Quietly.

Zen. I am Zen.

I remembered Census. Sitting in an uncomfortable plastic chair, sweating bullets and praying that Mal's amulets and spells would keep my charge from surging. Ignoring the itching beneath the wig that concealed my singed scalp. Answering questions for an Emerald Mage while another, lesser mage typed my responses.

After, I'd been left alone for close to an hour before the Emerald—a kind-faced woman who reminded me of Betty Crocker—had reentered and proclaimed me a cipher.

And I also remembered the two-way glass in the room.

"He was watching that day," I guessed. Adam nodded. "He recognized me. Alisande says I look like my mother."

"You do."

"So he kept tabs on me for four years, then when Gabriella disappeared, he started stalking me?"

"I wouldn't say that, exactly," he said dryly. "More like he began monitoring you more closely."

My throat was dry as dust as I swallowed the lump in it. "And here I'd always thought I was free, when I simply couldn't see the prison walls."

He said gently, "Perhaps it's not captivity but fate. The road set before you by forces unknown."

The fault lines of my world stretched, opening a void beneath my feet. I stared into Adam's eyes until everything else drifted away. And I suddenly knew, with absolute conviction, that he'd kept the worst from me.

"What else did my mother tell him, Adam?" He began shaking his head, but I grabbed him by the collar of his sweatshirt and yanked our faces close. "What. Else."

He didn't even try to fight me, eyes staying brown and anguished. In a broken voice, he whispered, "That you would bring his love back to life."

I recoiled in astonishment. "Gabriella?"

"Yes."

But it wasn't Adam who said it.

It was the Prime, standing in the doorway leading back into the compound, watching us with cool, blank eyes.

"That's insane," I blurted. "I can't raise the dead. I can't see the future."

"Not insane, merely extraordinary," he said mildly, "and if you are anything, you are that. Your mother spoke only the truth when Seeing. I don't know how you'll manage it, but you will bring Gabriella back."

I looked helplessly at Adam, but he was watching the Prime with sorrow. "I'm sorry. She needed to know."

The Prime nodded. "Yes, she did." He turned on his heel, then spoke over his shoulder, "We leave for the gala in two hours. Be ready."

He was gone.

Adam rose and the shimmering barrier of magic dissipated. Freezing air rushed around me, stinging my eyes and burning down my throat.

"I don't believe that's what Delilah meant by her message."

I took in Adam's fierce expression. Immediately, I began shaking my head. "You can't mean—"

"That's exactly what I mean. As I said before, you're completely unlike Gabriella. You're strong, brave, and direct. And I've seen the way you look at him."

"The way I look at him?" I bleated. "Adam, he has enough glamour to enter the Miss Universe contest and win. I look at him the same way everyone does."

If stares could level a person, I would've been flat on my back. Adam rasped, "His glamour is inactive for you, Fiona. *Inactive.* To protect you, he holds back his aura and therefore his glamour. You see him as a man. I don't know if anyone does that. Has *ever* done that."

I gave an incredulous snort-laugh. "No, that's not... I don't—bullshit."

Adam tilted his head. "And you possess a power even the Liberati cannot combat." He paused. "You killed a cipher, Fiona. With power. It's against the nature of their Ascension."

"Well, I'm not a mage, vamp, or shifter. I don't know what I am, besides stuck in the middle of the most epic clusterfuck ever."

Adam gave a weary laugh. "I wish I had answers for you, could teach you as I would a mage. If only..."

"Don't say it," I warned, standing and rubbing my arms against the cold. "I want nothing to do with Delilah Greer." He nodded stoically, and we walked side by side toward the compound. As we neared the door, I asked, "Do you really believe everything she said?"

He paused, a muscle ticking in his jaw, and wouldn't meet my eyes. "I didn't, not really, until last night." He finally looked at me. "You could have run. Instead, you fought. But it's more than that. It's the way Declan reacts to you, as an alpha to shifter. The way I feel toward you, as a perpetually annoyed older brother." I rolled my eyes and he smiled slightly. "And it's the way Connor behaves in your presence. No one, not even Gabriella, has ever penetrated his emotional defenses like you do. He cares for you. And it frightens him."

Anxiety stirred in the vicinity of my heart. "You're not psychic."

"No, but it doesn't take a psychic to know that Connor hasn't laughed in years like he has in the last week."

I shook my head sadly. Now that my blinders were off and I was aware of my burgeoning case of captor-worship, I wasn't about to let his words penetrate my newly constructed Connor Defense System.

"I'm sorry, Adam. I know you think it's some sign or whatever, but it's not. I'm a shiny new toy. Nothing more."

He looked deeply into my eyes and finally nodded. "All right." He gestured me through the door and we strode down an empty hallway toward the central hall.

"About tonight," I said at length. "If I'm supposed to be a member of the Prime's security detail, does that mean I get a gun? And for that matter, why don't you guys pack heat and just *shoot* the Liberati?"

Adam's lips twitched. "First of all, if we'd suspected a trap was waiting in Snoqualmie, we would have brought a small army of—yes—men who carry guns. Secondly, guns can be temperamental if enough magic is in the air. And thirdly, do you even know how to shoot one?"

"Hello? Daughter of an LAPD detective. I've been shooting guns since I could walk."

"Charming."

"That's what you pay me for, right?"

This time, he laughed. I grinned, feeling proud of myself, and nudged his shoulder lightly with mine.

"I've grown on you."

"Like a fungus," he muttered.

"Like a sister, you mean. So, are we friends now? Because if we're friends, I have to tell you how silly those white robes are. Unless you want to change your name to Wizard Gibbs."

He groaned.

15

MY SECURITY OUTFIT didn't come with a gun. It wasn't even practical: a floor-length, black sequined gown with a cut that made wearing a bra impossible, and a pair of heels that would break me if I tried to run but might be useful for poking someone's eye out.

Not until I joined Declan and seven other tuxedoed werewolves in the second of two limos outside the compound did I understand that my addition to the Prime's security detail was about appearance, not firepower.

"Good Lord," grumbled Declan, glancing at me askance as the limo pulled out of the circular drive. "Who the hell picked out that dress?"

I crossed my arms over my partially exposed chest, scowling at him. "It's not like I had a choice. A team of stylists was waiting for me in my room. I tried to run but this one lady—I think she was a werebear—tackled me. Three of them had to hold me down to get curlers in my hair."

The other werewolves laughed.

Declan did not.

"What happened today?" he asked mutedly.

I looked away. "Nothing. Everything's good."

"I see right through that crap," he said, albeit gently.

I see every layer of your mind and heart.

"I don't want to talk about it," I said, but softened the words by squeezing his hand, resting beside mine on the seat. "Let's boil it down to worry for my dad."

He threaded our fingers together, his grip reassuringly tight. "Okay."

I nodded thanks, ignoring the pointed focus of the other werewolves. Declan, though, wasn't having it. The pulse of his aura increased and a tickling growl filled his chest. From the corner of my eye, I watched the men begin inspecting their fingernails, adjusting their bow ties, and generally pretending they didn't see their alpha holding hands with a freaky, white-haired anomaly.

It was a half-hour drive to our downtown destination. I spent the time listening to the brotherly banter between wolves, and not thinking about the events of the day.

I wasn't thinking about it.

Nope, not thinking about Connor's dead girlfriend, my missing dad, and my psycho—I mean *psychic*—mother. I definitely wasn't thinking about her proclamation that I would bring Connor's love back to life. Or that Adam had tried to plant a matchmaking seed. Or that I was psychic, too.

Goddammit.

I wanted to go home.

When the limo rolled to a stop outside a glitzy hotel entrance and I saw paparazzi and reporters crowding either side of a red carpet, I almost threw up. As it was, I nearly bloodied Declan's hand with my fingernails.

"Are you kidding me?" I hissed.

Declan grinned as the door was opened from the outside. "What, you thought the designer dress was for a tea party?" He laughed at the mutinous expression on my face. "Just don't trip."

It was actually a near thing, prevented at the last moment by two of the wolves, who managed to keep me upright without making it look like I'd almost eaten carpet.

"Thanks," I whispered, which earned me a wink and a grin.

When the nine of us were unloaded and dramatically lining the curb, the first limo's doors finally opened. Samantha came first, resplendent in a pale blue gown that perfectly contoured her waifish physique. Her blond hair was bound in an elegant chignon, her makeup dramatic yet tasteful. She gazed imperiously at the crowd, a small smile on her face.

Behind her, the Prime emerged, and the paparazzi erupted.

"Prime Thorne!"

"Prime!"

"Connor!"

On and on, they yelled for him. For a look, a smile. I stuck close to Declan, not allowing myself my own look. A tuxedo was probably on par with a gladiator costume—detrimental if not immediately fatal to my IQ.

The red carpet was empty of other parties, no doubt intentionally, as no one stood a chance of winning the spotlight from the Prime.

Adam, white-robed and stoic, joined Declan and me as we brought up the rear. The rest of the wolves formed a loose vanguard before the power couple.

When Connor stopped for the fifth time to speak with a journalist, I whispered tensely, "How long is this going to take?"

Adam muttered, "As long as it takes."

We'd moved maybe another three feet when I heard the first murmurs. A moment later, I saw a finger pointing at me.

"Lightning..."

"Her hair..."

"Saved the Prime..."

"Fiona! Fiona!"

Declan's warm palm pressed to my bare back. "Smile, sparky. And breathe. You're hyperventilating."

My eyes moved of their own volition to the Prime. He was staring right at me, ignoring the yammering journalist behind him. His gaze flickered briefly down my dress, then snapped back to my face. He drew a breath, eyes flickering between peridot and emerald. Beside him, Samantha's lips thinned and an angry flush flooded her cheeks.

"Huh," said Declan.

And because timing was everything, and my life couldn't possibly get better, my arms began to itch.

I turned to Declan. "Get me inside, now. And don't touch me."

At some unspoken command from their alpha, the wolves split formation, allowing us a straight shot to the hotel's open doors. I squared my shoulders, focused on not tripping in my ridiculous heels, and sauntered inside without a backward glance. As soon as I entered the lobby, I veered toward the universal symbol for restrooms, passing through a glittering, whispering crowd.

The whispering grew louder, spiked with alarm, and those in my path hurried to get out of my way. A glance down at my arms told me why.

I rushed into the women's restroom, which was blessedly empty. As the door whooshed closed, I placed my palms flat on either side of a marble sink, drew a deep breath, and released it slowly. Then I did it again. And again, until Adam's bracelets cooled, my arms returned to pale with a sheen of scarring, and my charge equalized.

"I've been known to have bad ideas from time to time."

The mirror showed me the Prime leaning casually against the closed door. I straightened and pretended to fix my hair. Against the loose white curls, my dark brows and eyelashes stood out starkly. Samantha was right—I should invest in a wig. I looked like a comic-book character.

Continuing to fuss with nonexistent frizz, I avoided the Prime's gaze, unsure of where we stood with each other. The smarmy combativeness of our relationship thus far had clearly crossed some boundaries. For both of us.

With the reprimand in the training room fresh in my memory, I figured polite deference was the safest course.

"Thank you for checking on me. I'll be out in a minute."

"I can have Declan take you home, if you'd like."

I bit my tongue in restraint, temper flaring at both his empty, formal tone and the word *home*. It took a few more deep breaths, but when I finally turned to face him, I was calm. I even managed a smile.

"I'm fine now."

"Very well." He began to turn, then paused. "You'll be left to your own devices tonight, Fiona. Don't make me regret it."

"I won't," I said obediently.

He nodded, then disappeared. The door swung gently closed.

I turned back to the mirror to touch up my lip gloss, ignoring the feeling of having lost something I hadn't known was treasured.

THE GALA WAS DEFINITELY NOT my scene. There was too much flashy jewelry, too many fake tans, and an excess of overly bright teeth. Besides continuous, unsubtle gestures and murmurs about me, the Prime was right. I was left to my own devices.

At least the buffet was good.

From the banners hung to either side of a distant stage, apparently we were here to celebrate the reopening of several historic properties in downtown Seattle. It all seemed a little contrived to me, merely an excuse for the rich and powerful to rub elbows.

The Prime was no exception. From my table at the farthest edge of the ballroom, I watched him network. Women and men alike fawned over him, brought him cocktails, and touched him at every opportunity. Samantha never strayed from his side, a perfect accessory.

I wondered if she knew she was temporary, that Connor was waiting for Gabriella to return. For me to bring her back to life.

"Those don't look like pleasant thoughts."

I looked up at the man standing beside my table, a glass of wine in one hand. He was permanently in his mid to late thirties and handsome, tall and broad-shouldered, with olive skin, dark eyes, and a killer smile that was currently directed at me.

Barely visible around him was a sapphire aura, shot through with peculiar ribbons of violet. I'd never seen anything like it.

He tolerated my blatant study, and even smiled wider as he presented his hand to me.

"Fiona Sullivan, it's a pleasure to meet you."

I eyed his fingers. "Are you sure you want to risk it?" I asked, glancing pointedly at the buffer of space between my table and the crowd. The isolation was fine by me. All the auras in the room were giving me a headache.

He laughed. "Quite sure."

I shook his hand without incident. "You have me at a disadvantage."

Still smiling, he nodded at a chair several spaces from mine. "May I?" I nodded, and he unbuttoned his tux jacket and sat with lazy grace that reminded me, unfortunately, of Connor. "My name is Ethan Accosi. I'm a longtime associate of the Primes' Office."

"That's a rather vague job description," I said, cocking an eyebrow.

"Indeed," he said with a grin. "I think of myself as a silent partner in the struggle for balance between species."

"That, coming from someone whose species comprises the highest percentage worldwide? Nearly forty-eight percent, if I'm not mistaken."

His gaze stayed steady. "You're an incredibly beautiful woman, Fiona."

The compliment, and its tone of unreserved sincerity, affected me more than I cared to admit. Sending out a prayer of gratitude for my dad's weekly poker nights, I maintained a neutral expression.

"And you, Mr. Accosi, are skilled at redirection."

He chuckled. "And how is our favorite Prime treating his newest acquisition?"

"Extremely well," I said steadily.

"That's not what I've heard." A business card slid across the tablecloth. "If your feelings change, call me. Prime Kilpatrick would very much enjoy meeting you."

I reached for the card, but paused as I noticed the palest of violet shimmers radiating from it. Retracting my hand, I narrowed my eyes on my companion. "Seriously?"

He smiled with unfeigned delight. "So it's true."

"What?" I snapped, my stomach turning.

"You see magic." He glanced over my head and his smile turned sharp. "Is it also true, the rumor of where she sleeps at night?"

I stiffened as cool fingers trailed across my bare shoulder. Connor said silkily, "Tell Ian that his interest in Fiona is appreciated, but she's happy here. Isn't that right, *mo spréach*?" Fingertips teased the hair over my ear and my eyes went a little crossed.

"Yes," I whispered, then cleared my throat, heat rising to my face. So much for poker nights. "Yes. Thank you, Mr. Accosi."

Ethan was no longer smiling as he stood and offered a stiff nod. "Enjoy the rest of your evening," he said and strode away.

I turned in my seat, dislodging Connor's touch, and glared at him. "I thought we established that I can take care of myself, Prime Thorne."

He smiled slightly, without mirth, at my use of the honorific. "Did you notice his aura?"

I frowned. "Yes. I've never seen anything like it. Sapphire and violet."

"He's in the final stage before transition to Opal. Already a formidable mage, he will soon become Adam's equal."

"And he works for the Southern Prime?"

"Not exclusively. He's worked for me as well, once or twice. Ethan is an equal opportunity contractor." His gaze lifted over my head and went distant. "Were you tempted, Fiona?"

"By what? A spelled business card that would have done God knows what to me?" I shuddered. "No. I wasn't tempted."

His gaze lowered to my face. "There will be more offers. Ones I cannot match."

I slid from the chair and stood, needing to even the playing field a bit. Even with the heels, he was still a good two inches taller than me, but at least I wasn't craning my neck anymore.

"I'm here, with you, for one reason only," I said firmly. "To find my dad. When I do, I'm going back to my life. Until then, I'd appreciate it if you stopped touching me so familiarly. This hot and cold routine is giving me whiplash." Out of the corner of my eye, I saw Samantha heading our way. "You're date is waiting, Prime Thorne."

"Whiplash?" he asked, lips twitching.

The sight of his almost-smile was like a ray of sunlight piercing the clouds. My expression must have given something away, because Connor froze, then turned and walked away.

"Whiplash," I whispered to myself and went in search of fresh air.

16

THE STORM SIMMERING the past few days had finally boiled over. As I stepped onto a covered terrace on the second story of the hotel, a gust of wet air hit me in the face before the wind shifted, driving the downpour away from stone balustrades. Shivering, I crossed to the southwest corner, as yet spared the wind's notice.

The rain fell in sheets, thick and urgent. On the street below, headlights and taillights diffused into refractive blurs against the adjacent buildings and sidewalks. A distant flash of brightness in the sky was followed by a clap of thunder.

My arms tingled.

Live to be free, whispered the memory of my dad.

"You're in pain."

My heart catapulted into my throat as I spun to

face Ethan Accosi. His aura was a dim glow around his shoulders, bathing his features in a sinister light. His posture, at least, was nonthreatening, hands tucked into pockets as he leaned against the opposite railing.

"I'm fine," I said shortly.

"You're shackled, Fiona. Virtually imprisoned by the Omega."

"There are reasons," I said with a calm I didn't feel. "What do you want, Mr. Accosi?"

"Call me Ethan."

I nodded. "Fine."

He smiled and pushed off the railing, closing the distance between us with measured strides. The shoulders of his tux were wet from the rain, but he didn't seem to notice or care.

I had the sudden premonition that this conversation wasn't going to end well and eyed the door, estimating how many steps it would take to get there. And while I didn't truly think Ethan meant me harm, I nevertheless crossed my arms, angling my fingers beneath my wrists. Just in case.

"What do you want, Ethan?" I repeated.

"I want what everyone wants," he said with a small smile. "Knowledge. Power."

"Let me rephrase. What do you want from *me*?"

He halted several feet away, the intent in his gaze

warming my face. "I'd like very much for us to be allies. Unfortunately, I don't see that happening today. Just remember that what I do, I do for the good of humanity."

"What—"

"Your mother sends her regards."

His hands whipped from his pockets and I pressed the releases on my bracelets a second too late. I glimpsed a test-tube right before clear liquid hit me full in the face, steaming on impact with my charged skin.

I tasted... *licorice?*

Dragging my fingers over my eyes, I blinked at Ethan. "What the hell was that?"

"Just relax," he said, a strange, echoing quality to his voice. "It will be over in a minute."

The spell hit.

I staggered as white-hot pain pierced my temple, tearing a ragged moan from my throat. My knees buckled and I hit the terrace floor, my ankle twisting with a *pop*. The breath was knocked from my lungs. Animal noises of misery met my ears; dimly, I realized they were coming from me.

My vision spiraled and went dark, then burst into precision.

I saw Connor in the ballroom. He was dancing with Samantha, a detached expression on his face.

The real-time image flickered to Declan, who glanced at his watch before looking toward the stairs. Another flicker, then Adam, stiff and bored, speaking with a nameless man.

My vision blurred, then reset.

I saw Mal, pouring over texts in the Prime's library. Then my father's secretary, Rosie, driving a car on a dark highway, singing along to country music.

I saw my mother, her face as familiar as the one I saw in the mirror.

She was smiling.

"Live to be free, Fiona," she whispered.

Another excruciating bolt of pain tore through me. I felt myself being lifted, unable to fight, barely able to breathe.

"It will be over soon," said Ethan, his voice coming from the end of a long tunnel. "You'll never be shackled again."

I dragged air into my lungs and screamed, "CONNOR!"

His name brought me focus and I saw him again. His head whipped up, green irises blowing black. Then he was gone, and Samantha gasped, her dress swirling and arms hanging suspended around the space he'd occupied.

The door of the terrace blew off its hinges, smashing into the railing ten feet away.

"What have you done?" snarled the Prime, his voice dark as midnight, his power a leviathan—endless, radiant space. I writhed at the smothering magnitude of it and wondered if I was about to die. Or if my brain was already fried.

"I've freed her," said Ethan breathlessly.

Connor growled, "If you want to live another second, you'll give her to me."

I moaned as my body passed between the men. Pain flared, bowing my back with a convulsion. Ethan said, "She said it would be difficult, but I didn't know—"

Adam's Opal aura blew across the terrace like a wind, warm and vibrant. "What did you give her?" he demanded.

"Forgive me, Fiona," whispered Ethan.

Sapphire and violet lights blinded me and when they dimmed, the mage was gone.

"Fiona," said Connor. "Open your eyes."

I couldn't.

Instead, I thought of Ethan and saw him.

He strode swiftly down the street to a dark sedan. Opening the passenger door, he slid inside and looked across at the driver. She was a pale, dark-haired woman with striking eyes, clear blue and ringed with black lashes, crowned by graceful, sloping brows.

"Thank you," said my mother.

Ethan nodded. "You didn't tell me it would hurt her."

She put the car in gear and pulled smoothly into traffic. "Pain is a cornerstone of growth. She is strong. She will survive it and be even stronger."

"Adam, do something!"

"The bracelets aren't working. I can't touch her. Get her out of here before she blows this place apart!"

Cold wind.

Pelting rain.

The sky exploded—I exploded.

Freedom... then nothing.

17

I DREAMED of a sun-drenched glade in a forest. Butterflies fluttered and dove, iridescent wings shimmering. Wildflowers bloomed in riotous patches on the verdant ground. The sky was pale blue, crystalline and tinged with violet.

I felt him first, then turned and saw him.

He looked tired. His hair was mussed, tuxedo jacket missing, and bow tie hanging loose. The pale green eyes held an odd, desperate light. I took an uncertain step toward him. "What is it? What's happened?"

Connor shook his head minutely. "You haven't stopped screaming for an hour."

I stilled. "What?"

He broke eye contact, tilting his head to gaze at

the dream-sky. I stared at the strong column of his throat and remembered.

"Did you fry my brain with your aura?"

He huffed out a mirthless laugh. "No, but you're currently frying the ears of everyone in the compound."

"You're exaggerating," I breathed.

He looked at me. "Somewhat. Did Accosi say anything to you, before he hit you with the spell?"

It was my turn to look away. "Yes. He said my mother sent her regards." I paused, picking at my ruined dress. "I . . . I *saw* things. People. I saw Ethan get into a car with Delilah after he disappeared. Did she do what I think she did?"

"It seems that way."

I looked at him sharply. Instead of the relief or excitement I'd expected, there was only fatigue.

"Shouldn't you be happy? Your seeing-eye dog just earned her badge."

"Yes, I suppose I should be . . . happy. Perhaps I will be, once you stop screaming."

I winced. "Do you think the spell went wrong somehow?"

Connor shook his head. "You've been talking between incoherent shouts, sometimes details of the present, locations of people you know. Other times, vague tableaus of the future. Adam is recording it.

When you regain consciousness, and focus, you should only have to think of your father to find him."

Tears of relief stung my eyes, but my heart was strangely heavy. "I don't want this," I whispered. "I don't want to see the present, the future, any of it."

"Neither did your mother. Not at first."

"How did this happen?"

He seemed to understand what I was asking. "I'm not sure. If there'd been a spell in place keeping your ability suppressed, Adam would have sensed it by now. It's more likely you were born with the power, but it's been dormant all these years, not even awakening with Ascension. Knowing this, Delilah found a mage who could engineer the right type of spell."

My limbs felt weighted. I didn't fight the lethargy, letting my legs buckle and deposit me on the soft grass. I plucked at the blades near my hip, severing tiny stalks and tossing them aside.

"Have I said anything interesting about the future? Winning lottery numbers, maybe?"

"No," he said, so quickly that I looked up with narrowed eyes. "Nothing but disjointed ramblings. It was like that with Delilah, too, at least until her Ascension."

"Everything comes back to that woman, doesn't it?" I shook my head, communicating that I didn't want or expect a response. "Did she tell you what she is? Is there even a name for it?"

Connor lowered gracefully, propping himself on an arm and crossing his long legs at the ankle. He gazed at me with a fixed, solemn expression. It wasn't the dreaded blankness; almost, it was worse.

"As a former Statistician, can you accept that Ascension was an accident? A random occurrence with no definitive cause?"

"Hell no."

His lips curved slightly. "What popular theory do you ascribe to?"

"I don't think the truth has been discovered yet."

"Mmm." His smile grew. "Perhaps there were forces at work that cannot be quantified."

I snorted. "I'm a little surprised to hear the God angle from you."

His brows lifted. "Because vampires are damned, hellish creatures? I have a soul, *mo spréach*."

I couldn't hold his gaze, so I stared at a nearby tree, tracing veins of moss on its pale, peeling trunk.

He continued softly, "Supernatural powers existed in this world long before Ascension. Long before the first vampire, shifter, and mage. There are Fae races, mythic beasts, monsters of the sea . . . and before the concept of one God, there were many gods, and those gods procreated with mankind."

I stared at him. "Are you saying my mother thinks she's the daughter of god?"

"Not necessarily. I'm saying there are mysteries in this world that will never be discovered. In ancient India, Indra was the god of lightning. In Rome, it was Zeus. In Greece, Jupiter. In Norse mythology it was Thor, son of Odin. The concept of beings holding elemental powers is not new."

"You've lost me," I said weakly.

"There are gods of fire, of the sea, of the earth . . . Masters of the elements. You were struck by lightning and survived, Fiona. You hold its destructive power in your hands, control it, channel it. You're not a vampire, shifter, or mage, but you are supernatural. Maybe you are the progeny of godkind. Maybe you are not."

"Wow. Just . . .wow."

He smiled softly. "It is the same with prophetesses. Oracles, Sibyls, Seers, Visionaries. They've peppered the timeline of the world, noted in nearly every culture. Rare creatures, who see the warp and weft of time, the tapestry of future days as it is being woven. There's no telling what culmination of genetics and fate birthed you." He paused. "Nor can we know the secrets Delilah keeps."

My spine stiffened. "If you're implying what I

think you are, you can stop right there. I'm Frank Sullivan's daughter."

Those solemn eyes just watched me. Patient. Gentle.

"Enough, Connor," I whispered. "Enough."

I jerked at his sudden presence on his knees before me, then froze as he caught my first tear with the pad of his thumb. And when his palm grazed my jaw, and his fingers sank into my hair, the world went soft and hazy.

I had the nebulous thought that this moment had already been written. That everything was exactly as it should be, each second a culmination of all seconds before and after, and the present but a small thread in a tapestry of infinite scope.

He said my name.

Cool, soft lips pressed onto my closed eyelids, the tip of my nose, and each cheek. Long fingers held my face gently. So gently.

When his lips grazed mine, electricity veered from my body in small *snaps* of sound, and I finally understood the danger that was Connor Thorne.

I wanted him. Mind, body, and spirit. As naturally as a flower wants sunlight, as inherently as every living creature's desire to live. To feel and rejoice.

Shadows blotted out the sun overhead, and a name filtered through my mind.

Gabriella.

"No," I said, jerking back and scrambling to my feet.

He whispered my name on a small, broken exhale. I memorized his expression—vulnerable, naked with desire for me. Only me. Then I packed it away for a rainy day and straightened my spine.

"Get out of my head, Connor."

He vanished.

The glade vanished.

I was alone. And empty.

*Thank you for reading **Ascension**. The story continues in **Reckoning**, Book 2 of the Ascension Series…*

Visit Laura Hall on Amazon

ABOUT THE AUTHOR

Laura Hall is the alter-ego of contemporary romance author, L.M. Halloran. When not writing or reading, the author can be found gardening barefoot or chasing her spirited daughter. Some of her favorite things are puzzles, podcasts, and small dogs that resemble Ewoks.

Home is Portland, Oregon.

authorlaurahall@gmail.com
authorlaurahall.com

ALSO BY LAURA HALL

THE ASCENSION SERIES

Ascension

Forthcoming

Reckoning

Unraveling

Rebirth

Tribulation

To stay informed of new releases,

follow Laura Hall on Amazon.

Printed in Great Britain
by Amazon